GOOD – BU

Good – But Hot

ANTOINE DE CAUNES

●

Translated by

LIZ HERON

FOURTH ESTATE · London

First published by Fleuve Noir

First published in Great Britain in 1991 by
FOURTH ESTATE LIMITED
289 Westbourne Grove
London W11 2QA

ISBN 1-872180-29-9

Typeset by York House Typographic Ltd., London
Printed in Great Britain by Biddles Ltd., Guildford

For Agnès

If it's funny, it's a joke
If it's not funny, it's a story.

(OLD TEXAN SAYING)

Foreword

I met Sam Murchison in a New York bar at the end of the seventies, by an extraordinary fluke. There I was sitting quietly at the bar, going through the sports pages of the *New York Post*, sipping a whisky, when a guy came and sat down next to me, ordered the same drink and unfolded the same newspaper at the same page. This coincidence made me smile, and when he noticed the reason for my amusement he started wisecracking about there being nothing like the kicks you get from combining an interest in booze and sport.

This was how we began a wonderful conversation that, as words and years went by, gradually turned into a solid and loyal friendship.

And believe me, I don't use the word lightly. Both of us, Sam and me, hardly ever use it, so we don't debase its true value.

When on each of my trips to New York we would regularly meet up at the same place, he started filling me in on some of his exploits. I listened, for hours on end, fascinated by these stories, all of them equally amazing, until the day I suggested writing them down and having them published, under his complete control of course. He held back for a long time, until the day he wound up accepting my proposal, with the argument that even if it's wasting people's time, it might as well be with a book like this than with – to quote him – 'some tedious tome on the future of monogamy, mid-life crisis in middle management, or any other crap like that'.

From that day on I applied myself to keeping an almost obsessive record of every word he said, down to his perpetual delight in listing everything he drinks, eats or wears.

All in all, our friendship has gone from strength to strength, without ever getting in the way of our differences.

I'm no Sam Murchison, though I can acknowledge I'm very proud of the trust he has placed in me, and I feel I haven't betrayed it.

ONE

I didn't have toothache when I got up that morning. In fact I didn't ache anywhere. On the other hand, I was feeling excruciatingly irritated by the sneaky lead pipes that were boring right through my skull with quite unimaginable cruelty. Kind of like a gang of bulldozers had, for the fun of it, been laying a trans-Amazon pipeline to connect my right ear with my left carotid artery, and back again while I slept. And clearly the liver region was just too good to be missed out. I had the distinct impression a squadron of marines had spent the night using it for target practice. I knew for sure that I was still alive, but I swear to God every single bullet had scored a bull's-eye. In short, I was paying the price – and everything down here has a price – for the big mickey of Black Label whisky I had knocked back the night before with my buddy Joe.

Nothing strange about that, I have to admit. But waking up like this makes you realise you won't see twenty again, and the bill will just go on getting steeper. On top of it all, there was a smartass sun playing around with my venetian blinds, sending out little 2,000-watt bolts that hit me right in the left eye, the one that happened to be more bloodshot.

Being a private eye in New York has its charm. Each new day brings its share of little adventures. You get to rub shoulders with some pretty interesting specimens of the species you and I – especially you – are members of. You can even get to travel around, but don't count on it for piling up that nest egg to pay for a second Chrysler Building. I'm not saying private eyes are all misers who only leave tips on Sundays, but . . . Take my office for example. A good location, south-facing, on the fourteenth floor of a building near the corner of 45th and Broadway. I've got a nice sign, with gold lettering on a glass door, two offices with air conditioning and even a shower. But when it comes to soundproofing, it's nowhere. Okay, we get by. Sooner or later it reaches a point where the sirens, the non-stop drone of the traffic, even the hammering from the building site next door, finally dissolve into a soothing purr. You just have to be in a good mood. But that day, you'll have realised, I wasn't in a good mood.

I let myself trickle off the sofa the way you drain the oil from a can of sardines, and, with that morning after feeling, headed towards the shower and its healing waters. On the way there I could hear the reassuring tap-tap of Belinda's Remington. Belinda's my secretary. She's been working for me for seven years and I can only say she's a paragon. Not exactly pretty, not exactly ugly either, and she has always demonstrated the kind of devotion bordering on self-sacrifice that, in an ideal world, should be the attribute of any normal woman. If Belinda was already there tapping away at her keyboard, it meant it was after 10. Not much later, because she always woke me up by 11. With a remarkable degree of skill I shunted myself around the corner between our offices to push her door open a crack and croak, in a voice from beyond the grave:

2

– Get the coffee on.

– Morning, Sam, she answered in melodious tones, I hope you had a good sleep.

– Coma might be a better word, I quipped, only half in jest.

I closed the door again, with more delicacy than a munitions expert defusing a TNT charge, swivelled myself onto the opposite track and this time headed straight for the shower. I undressed, stepped on an entire family of cockroaches, set the pressure on atomic power and plunged straight under the avalanche of ice-cold water. It's a shock to the system, there's no denying it, but I haven't found a better cure yet. In a matter of minutes I had drowned last night and regained the fitness and dynamism that are a crucial part of my legendary reputation.

In no time I was dry. I helped myself to a freshly laundered shirt still in its Tonkin' dry cleaner's wrapping, put my gorgeous black suit back on, slipped my shoes on my tootsies and poured myself a large neat whisky, the perfect cure for a hangover, as any quack worthy of the name will tell you. I girded up my loins with my faithful friend, a classic Magnum 357 Smith & Wesson. It can get in the way when it comes to everyday life, but it's indispensable whenever there's a rhinoceros charging at you, something which, oddly enough, happens to me fairly often. A little fine tuning with the electric razor, and there I am as bright and bushy-tailed as I was before my last outing with good old Joe.

Belinda had a cup of steaming black coffee waiting for me, and I swallowed half of it in a single gulp to see if my throat could take it. The steel-cladding had stood up well.

– That's what I call coffee, Belinda my sweet, I pronounced.

– You're a tough man to fool, Sam, she parried with a smile. I'll have plenty of news for you once you're back among the living.

– Good or bad?

– A bit of both. Let's say a good mixture for now.

– I'm all ears, I coaxed, knocking back another two pints of Java.

– Claire Hopkins rang about the expenses claims for shadowing her husband. She was outraged that you had the gall to charge for a drive-in movie ticket in New Jersey. She says she didn't hire you to go to the movies and you could easily have waited for her husband outside.

– Tell her to relax. He wasn't cheating on anybody, just bored. It was a great movie. Screwing the good-looking blonde he was with would have been sacrilege in the middle of *Dirty Harry*.

– Sam! You know I hate that kind of talk.

– It's one of the few luxuries I have left, honey.

– Sergeant Muldaur of the 32nd Precinct would like to talk to you about Fabio Martini, an East Village pimp whose body was found two days ago. He says he's aware you don't mix socially with this kind of person, but he was amazed to find your favourite bullets, Hollow Point, along with, I think it was Metal Piercing, in Martini's stomach and spleen. He's wondering whether you didn't by any chance have a disagreement with this gentleman.

– Tell Stan I was nowhere near St Mark's Place the night before last at 9.45.

– How did you know that . . . ?

– I know everything, Belinda. That's why people pay me sometimes. What else?

– The City Tax Office confirms that you've sent them the form for the last six months' payments, but say you've neglected to put your cheque in the envelope.

– Again? That's getting to be a habit. All the same, I was sure . . . .

– Sam . . . you didn't even write the cheque . . . .

– Don't forget to remind me if I forget again, Belinda. You haven't told me about the good news?

– I'm nearly there. Just one little thing. Jack d'Annunzio, the owner of the Lone Star Café where you spent part of last night, reckons you owe him 120 dollars for the mirror you and your friend Joe used for a bottle throwing contest. He won't charge you for the bottles since they were empty.

– And the mirror was full, huh? 120 dollars!? For that price he'll be able to have electricity put in. Tell him I'll drop by.

– I've the distinct impression he isn't offering up any prayers for your return, Sam.

– What if we were to move on to the good news, I suggested.

– A certain Glenn Belmont, a Miami businessman, is staying in New York. He's heard of your connection with the Guilbert case. His daughter hasn't been in contact with him for the last two weeks. He was supposed to meet her in Manhattan, but the phone number she gave him doesn't exist. He'd like you to drop in and see him at his hotel at 6.30.

– Okay. You can confirm that. Which hotel?

– The Plaza.

– Is that it?

– That's it, Sam.

I took down the name and address, poured myself a fresh cup of coffee, and went back to my office, with a nod of thanks to Belinda. After opening the blinds to let in a little more light, I glanced down at the street; I pretended I couldn't hear the thudding of the sledge-hammer from next door, and lit my last Winston. I've always had a gift for doing two things at once. Fourteen floors below it was the usual zoo. Columns of demented ants all looking like they're in a hurry. Some striding along quickly, some even running; others standing by, limp, watching them stride and run. A lot of traffic, thousands of cars playing switch-back on the broken-up roads. Here and there a few clouds of steam rising from the underground ventilation systems; nothing out of the ordinary, in other words.

I had more or less resurfaced. My last case had been closed since the day before, and a new case was beckoning on the horizon for that very evening. I had nothing else to do except kill the ten hours or so between now and my appointment. And killing time in New York, when you're thirty-eight, not bad looking with nearly all your teeth (it's not just mirrors that get broken in bars) and you've been born with the gift of the gab – believe me, I've done harder things in my time.

I started with a quick call to Joe so he could share in my optimism for this beautiful day.

TWO

Joe Mangelson and me, you could say we were brothers. The fact that my name's Murchison isn't important. We met in the middle of 'Nam, at the end of the winter of '68. We were both in the 26th Marines, stationed at Khe Sahn, which resembled a hotplate being pounded night and day by Russian and Chinese artillery hidden under camouflage on the other side of the Laotian frontier, about six miles away. The kind of place where you think twice before dropping off to sleep, even if it's with one eye open, because nothing guarantees you'll be able to open either of them again, that's if you wake up at all. In short, it was war, a rotten, dirty war; you must have heard about it somewhere. And ever since that shit was invented, I've never heard of any memories it left behind that you could put to music.

In between the shelling and the automatic rifle fire, Joe and I discovered we had a lot of things in common. American football, baseball, girls, beer, and great music like Presley, Buddy Holly and Tamla Motown. We got out of Khe Sahn. We didn't look too great – I had an ugly wound in the stomach after hand-to-hand combat in the jungle, and Joe's back was riddled with

7

microscopic bits of scrap metal – but we were alive. Whatever anyone says, that's what matters. And then civilian life had us in its mitts again. Joe got into some multifarious trading activities, just on the wrong side of what's legal, while I set up my agency after a non-too scintillating slave at the Hunts Point Precinct in the Bronx as a sworn-in Inspector. When it came to team work and esprit de corps, I'd done my bit against the Reds. Back home I found that I needed to work alone without getting my fingers rapped at every turn just for having roughed up some two-bit mugger a little bit.

So, in a manner of speaking, Joe and I were on opposite sides of the fence, but our friendship had set natural boundaries on our respective areas of operation. For twelve years now we hadn't clashed in the slightest on the business side, nor on any other either. He had officially set up house with a little cutie called Ruth, and I'd stayed single, the only imaginable state for a guy like me.

When I rang his number I figured she'd answer. I was right. She started yelling at me.

– Sam Murchison, how many times do I have to tell you? I don't want you sending Joe home to me like that. Do you know what that moron did? He tried to come in through the kitchen door in his Buick, at 5 a.m., then spent the rest of the night up against the boiler, talking to it as if it was me. He even wanted it to

. . . .

– He went as far as confusing you with a boiler? In your place I'd be inclined to take that as a compliment, Ruth sweetheart.

– Maybe in winter, she said missing the point, it's not so nice in spring. Joe swore to me just a week ago that he would give up drinking between meals. And as soon as he sees you again he comes back pixilated.

– We were in the restaurant for a long time. The service is getting slower and slower at the Durango.

– Anyhow he's asleep. Unless it turns out to be a coma. And you'll do me the favour of leaving him in peace for a while.

– I only wanted to find out how he's doing, Ruth!

– He's doing very badly, thank you, she asserted, in a decidedly assertive tone of voice, as she hung up on me.

It's true I'd been a bit worried about him making it home last night, as I'd watched him head out towards Brooklyn Bridge back to his little house in Sheep's Head Bay. But he'd arrived safe and sound, that was the main thing, and I could easily call him at his office in the afternoon – that way I'd avoid flying debris from his touchy other half. Ruth is a terrific girl when she's in a nice mood, which happens on Christmas Eve and the day they leave on their vacation. But in the end, people choose their own ball and chain. I was Joe's buddy, but it didn't mean I was sentenced to helping his wife with the knitting after our weekend picnics.

I was just looking for a cigarette when I remembered my packet had bit the dust a few minutes ago. I decided to go out and stock up and get some chow at the same time. I went into the first Howard Johnson I came across off Times Square and ordered four fried eggs, sunny side up, some grilled ham, home fries on the side, two pancakes with bilberry jam, a double OJ and a few more pints of coffee. While an attractive waitress was passing on the order for my pleasure, never mind her own, I got a few decks of Winston from the machine and treated myself to the morning's

Post. The front page showed the somewhat contorted body of a pin-up. Her photographer boyfriend had had the idea of pushing her out of his studio window on the ninth floor, a move that has a tendency to prove fatal. And it had, yet again. I made a bee-line to the sports page and saw that the Dodgers had beat the Pittsburgh Pirates. Here was a good start to the day. With my stomach filled I decided to stroll up to Central Park. Then I treated myself to a couple of doughnuts, vanilla and chocolate, began to feel a whole lot better, and wound up coming in to land on the edge of the Park. I selected a bench as lonely as I was to sprawl out on under the lukewarm April sunshine. I hadn't even had the time to flick on my charm when a juicy babe came along and sat down on my left. She had an animal of some kind on a leash, much too small to be a bear and much too big to be a beaver. What's more, it was whimpering nastily.

The ball of fur was spinning round like a top gone berserk as it tried to catch its own tail, if a tail was in there.

– Change its batteries, I wisecracked, it's winding down.

Its owner looked me over idly and, no doubt impressed by my appearance and my irresistible smile, she seemed to relax.

– I hate this little horror, she confessed. But it's a present from Jimmy and he kinda thought I'd like it.

– Jimmy is a man with taste, I told her, meanwhile hastily extricating my shinbone, which the little horror had mistaken for a female of his species. At least as far as you're concerned.

– Thanks.

– It's my pleasure. Murchison. Sam Murchison.

– Hi, I'm Pamela Greenwood.

10

What you are is not at all bad, doll. That's what I felt like telling her. But I restrained myself. All the way from Texas in her Sunday best and lovely with it. I asked her if she was just visiting in New York.

– Yeah, more's the pity. We're stayin' at the Stanhope, a real good hotel. Do you know it?

– Of course, I lied. But I've heard that the food there's terrible.

– Oh yeah? What's wrong with it?

– The people who tried it have checked out so I can't ask them, but maybe we could leave Sultan with the cooks instead. I'm sure they'd know what to do with him. And that would leave us free to visit the bedrooms. Now *they've* got a good reputation.

She showed no sign of being shocked.

– That would be very nice, Mr Murtchison . . . .

– Mur-chi-son. Murchison.

– I'm sorry, but Jimmy's expecting me, and the thing is he's very jealous.

– That doesn't bother me, Pamela. I'm not the possessive type.

No way, it was out of the question. I felt like screwing her there and then on the grass behind the bench, but there would be twelve million witnesses ready to make the most of it and ruin my public image.

Since the lady was out of bounds I got up from the bench and took my leave.

– Life's a bitch, Pamela. Chance brings us together, chance forces us to part. See you around maybe.

– Maybe-ee, she concurred, with a smile no less irresistible than mine.

With that I left the bench, Sultan and his owner, all three in a state of high excitement, especially his owner. With a little sorrow in my heart, a little tickle in my loins, and the same feeling of promise unfulfilled that great artists sometimes have.

I went into a phone booth and called Joe at his office. He told me I was *persona non grata* at his house and that Ruth had pinned up an old Vietnam photo of me so she could get some darts practice.

I warned him we'd have to share the bill for the mirror – he had the nerve to ask what mirror? – and I said we should have another night on the town.

– Just let things simmer down for now, he begged.

I told him he'd be hearing from me soon, which was no surprise to him, then I went on my way past the Park. I went into a 57th Street cinema, just as twelve thousand Apaches were war dancing around a pretty blonde with perfect beehive, and, the hail of gunfire notwithstanding, I dozed off pronto.

I opened one eye at the precise moment when the same twelve thousand Indians were chorusing a war cry, and I looked at my watch. 6.10. I'd slept for two hours, all the way through the West being won, and I was still alive. I left the theatre at once, being careful not to wake up the seven people in the audience and not to step on too much popcorn, and headed for the Plaza.

In reception I asked for Mr Belmont and the clerk told me to wait in the Oyster Bar, one of the hotel's three high-class watering holes. Mr Belmont wouldn't be long. I settled onto a six-foot-high stool, ordered a double Jack Daniels neat, and tried to decipher the menu on the wall opposite me. I felt like a million bucks.

I'd just got nine-tenths of the way through with my left eye closed when I heard my name being spoken behind me. I made a sharp half turn and found myself face to face with a tubby guy going a bit grey on top,

12

just the kind of client who mislays his daughter and asks a peeper to find her for him.

– Mr Murchison?

– The very same, I confirmed.

– Delighted, Glenn Belmont, he said as we pressed the flesh. I'm grateful for your punctuality.

He managed to hoist himself onto a stool without the benefit of a winch, and signalled to the waiter.

– A Bloody Mary, Joseph. And make it a stiff one. Will you join me, Mr Murchison?

– Love to. (I've never understood this habit of drowning vodka in tomato juice.)

– Would you like some oysters? Belmont asked me. I'm kind of peckish myself, so I could eat a few. How about you?

– Hey, that's a good idea. They say it's very bad to drink on an empty stomach, I replied, worrying now that he was going to end up asking me to dance.

– Two dozen specials, Joseph, with vinegar sauce.

Here's one guy whose daughter's disappearance doesn't spoil his appetite, I thought to myself.

Having disposed of the orders, Belmont reached in his pocket and took out a solid gold cigarette case with his initials encrusted on it, offered me one of those extra mild brands for advanced cancer cases, which I politely refused, lit one himself with a black lacquered Cartier, inhaled and blew some smoke out, then decided to get straight to the point.

– Mr Murchison, I've come to you because your reputation has got as far as Miami, where I live most of the time. I run a business wholesaling coffee, Belmont Inc., and we supply two-thirds of the US market. I'm sixty-two, I have three children, two boys from a first marriage, and Maria-Liza, my nineteen-year-old daughter who's the child of my last marriage.

– That's what I call plain speaking.

– You'll know as well as I do, you've got to be straightforward to get things done.

– And Maria-Liza has run away, is that it?

– I don't know if that's how I'd put it. She's a sensible girl, she did brilliantly in her exams at the end of last year and my wife and I both thought we should give her a bit of time this year to decide what she wanted to do. We've got used to her going away for a few days at a time whenever she feels like it. But always keeping in touch with us. Well, it's two weeks now since we've heard a thing from her. I'm not getting over-anxious – she was seen here in New York just a few days ago by one of my employees. It turns out she's fallen for a rock musician who was visiting Miami with his band, and to all appearances she left with him. What I can't understand is that she hasn't even bothered to phone us.

– Why haven't you filed a missing persons notice? Funnily enough, a lot of people do get traced in New York.

– In the first place because Maria-Liza is a major, if only just. In the second place because her safety isn't at risk as far as I know, and I consider that a family matter with no public repercussions isn't the business of the police.

I was tipping back the dregs of my first drink and wondering if Belmont bought his clichés by the dozen, and whether he had a deal that gave him his money back if they misfired.

That was the moment Joseph the barman chose to present us with the Bloody Mary, my second whisky, and the twenty-four oysters selected for sacrifice along with the murder weapon in the shape of the

14

vinegar. What torment there must have been inside those shells.

– I understand, I said, acquiescent, silently blessing the acephalous molluscs, hermaphrodites all.

– How long do you think it'll take to find Maria-Liza, assuming she's still in New York? Belmont asked me, gulping down oyster number seven, after a squirt of acid.

– If all goes well I ought to be able to bring her back to you in a week, ten days max, I exaggerated. That's taking for granted, as you say, that she really is in New York. Do you know what I charge, Mr Belmont?

– Money's no problem.

That's the kind of answer I really like.

– I'd rather make things quite clear. It's a question of principle. It'll be 250 dollars a day, plus expenses, I told him, dowsing an unsuspecting number fifteen in my turn.

The oyster jumped, Belmont didn't.

– That's fine by me, he said, his eyes still glued to one of his victims.

– Looks like the oyster doesn't see it that way, I wisecracked, pointing at it cowering back inside the shell.

Belmont rewarded me with a mechanical smile.

– Maybe you'd like to see a photo of Maria-Liza?

– I was going to ask you for one.

He swallowed half of his Bloody Mary, and dried his fingers on one of the scented napkins, then he pulled out a wallet that would have given the average Queens mugger heart failure, and removed a photograph tucked behind gold credit cards. When he slid this portrait in front of me I nearly let out a little wolf whistle, but I just managed to hold myself back. If I

15

kept on holding myself back like that I'd never be in any danger of falling.

– She's very pretty, I assured him.

– I know, and she knows it.

– If she acknowledges it, then it means she's not altogether unaware – I tried to be reassuring.

Maria-Liza was framed by a photographer who'd stopped short just below the bust. A lovely bust, you could say that all right. Unfortunately hidden under a black sweater that was stretched tight. Almond eyes, light-coloured and probably blue; a nose Bette Midler would envy; full, generous lips that revealed a keyboard neater than a Steinway's, only without the black keys; the ensemble set off by dark hair that had a light curl. If the bottom half was as good as the top half, she was a sure-fire Delilah. I pulled myself together.

– In what part of the city was she seen, Mr Belmont?

– At the corner of Third Avenue and 21st Street; she was coming out of Tiffany's coffee shop, the distraught father replied swallowing numbers ten, four and nine in quick succession. The pace was getting to be too much for me.

– Do you know the name of the band the musician plays in? I asked, making a quick play for number nineteen, which was particularly fat and all the more sacred.

– It's a weird name, said Belmont, rummaging through his credit card suitcase and extracting a piece of paper: the Last Chance Band.

– The last band before the desert, I wisecracked.

– Find her for me, Mr Murchison, find her. Her mother's upset as hell about it (most probably another doll) and she made me swear to bring Maria-Liza back to Miami this weekend.

It was Monday.

16

– I'll do my best. There's still the question of whether Maria-Liza agrees to go home. There's nothing to suggest she will.

– She MUST come home, Mr Murchison, insisted Belmont, with renewed authority.

– Where can I reach you this week?

– I'm making the most of my stay in New York to settle some business. I'll be staying at the Plaza until Wednesday. Then it'll be my office or my home in Miami, he said, offering me the latest card from his collection.

I put this little item in my pocket, gulped down the last of my second drink, gave him my renewed assurance of a speedy solution to the problem, and left him alone with Joseph and the horrified survivors.

– Mr Murchison, he called out just as I reached the door of the bar, she's still just a child.

A child with promise, I thought without turning – it's tricky, but I manage it fairly well – and simultaneously making a backward gesture of assent, in keeping with the anxieties of a lawful father.

THREE

When I left the Plaza I flagged down a taxi and gave the address of my office to a driver called Salomon Jackubowicz, a Polish refugee who appeared to have crossed the Iron Curtain and a few minefields in this old heap, judging by the suspension. I lit up, which gave the Polack a few ideas about red lights, and went back to thinking about Belmont, a guy who spent his life having fires lit under tons of coffee that would over-stimulate entire populations. It was clear that the disappearance of one of his heirs wasn't making him lose any sleep at night. What was eating him wasn't so much that she'd gone off to have a fling with a pretty boy, more that she hadn't bothered to let him know. It was lousy manners, but since he was the one who'd raised her he knew all too well who to blame. Probably that accounted for his coolness. Instead it was the missus who was worrying. My baby Maria-Liza, left to fend for herself in the modern jungle, and all that baloney. On the other hand, if it was really the first time she'd run away, there was no mystery about it. Either she was crazy about her prince charming, or else she wanted to teach a lesson to parents who were cramping her style, or maybe

18

weren't around enough. I had too little to go on to work it out yet.

When we drew up at my building I gave a princely tip of 25 cents to Jackubowicz, then I bought the latest *Village Voice* from the kiosk. The front page was asking the vexing question: 'Can You Be Gay And A Republican?', which gave the impression that the Democrats were all fags, but nobody's perfect.

Belinda had already gone, leaving a prominent message on my desk: 'Nancy Belmont rang from Miami at 6 o'clock, before you were due to meet her husband. She's very keen for you to handle this case. She wants you to call her this evening at her home, collect if necessary – it's necessary, isn't it, Sam dear! She wants to fill you in on a few things. She seemed quite upset. I hope you've recovered from your last bender and remain yours ever, Belinda.

P.S. The number: (305) 471 1583.'

I lit another cigarette, since the last one had had it, took off my jacket, relieved myself of my Smith & Wesson, sprawled out in my armchair – which had already worn out two generations of American posteriors – put up my feet on the corner of the desk, lifted the phone and asked the operator for the Florida number, collect, since it was necessary, at least in Belinda's eyes. The lines were busy and the operator told me I'd have to wait ten minutes or so. I lifted the *Voice*, opened it at the music page, and started scanning it for some mention of the Last Chance Band.

The listings were there all right, you only had to peer at them. I saved myself the trouble when I put the paper on my desk and found a staggering four pages full of display ads for hundreds of gigs, each of them classified for the benefit of connoisseurs. This was all Greek to me, labels like Psycho-Rockabilly, Hard Core

Punk, Heavy Metal Fusion, Neo-Funk Rap, Progress-ive Folk, to say nothing of Twist-Double-X and other alternative art-jazz stuff. All of it with no suggestion of a sell-by date. For immediate consumption.

When it came to music, as you may have gathered, I was still somewhere back with the basics, a kind of family tree with whites on one side and blacks on the other, or vice versa, according to taste. Sometimes it mixed nicely, but at any rate you always knew where you were. Now everything suggested that the family tree had become overgrown; it was vegetation with thousands of branches. I had known the bee's shade, now I was discovering the forest. It's little things like that that remind you how time is passing you by helter-skelter. I saw myself as Little Red Riding Hood with her dumb little pot of butter, surrounded by a pack of Howling Wolves. What made it worse was that when all these kids got together in a band, the names they picked out for themselves were enough to scare off the last virgin in the free world – if there were any left. They made you shudder; things like: the Fourth Reich, Angel Fuckers, the Dead Kennedys, Motorhead, Supertramp, Killing Joke, the Cramps, and other gems. I wondered if this entire little world was created behind barbed wire, or whether protec-tive helmets were compulsory for the audience, but in the end it was kind of funny. Things had just changed such an awful lot since my day, a viewpoint I share with a good many observant folk. In the sixties, all a rock singer had to do was claim that, by comparison with his own, Jesus Christ's reputation was worth no more than a bottle of mineral water in a Texan diner, and the self-appointed guardians of morality would immediately be up in arms and yelling blasphemy. Since then, either morals had relaxed a bit, or the

Watch Committees had evaporated, just like the smelling salts they'd needed to revive them twenty years ago. Anyhow, I couldn't care less.

My mind was on all this stuff when my eyes suddenly hit on the notorious, albeit not yet famous name, Last Chance Band. They were being hyped under Latino Black and White Funk-Rock. And they had indeed been playing three nights before, in a midtown club, the Peppermint Lounge.

The short piece that went with the gig listing ran like this, word for word: 'Three years touring, two albums and four 45s bring us to this paradoxical conclusion: the Last Chance Band makes some of the best music you can hope to hear these days. They've remained true to their influences , blending them into their own compositions, and these fall nowhere short of their inspiration. They've come up with a sound that corresponds to the pulse of the eighties, halfway between the hot sensuality of electronic music and the affectlessness of the synthesiser. Joe de Brown sings better every day. Yet strangely it's that little something they lack to be truly original that makes for their success in Europe. As if the Last Chance Band was in a sense too ideally American for America. Close to parodying an image that borders on cliché, but high-class cliché. To be seen or seen again at all cost.'

Pithy stuff. In short, these guys liked the band, but at the same time they were saying there was no good reason to like it, and plenty of reason for it to go and be liked somewhere else. It had to be the new approach to reviewing in this neck of the woods. I was lost in these musings when the telephone's ring made me start. I hate answering the phone when it rings, but I was waiting for a call so I lifted the receiver at once.

21

– Your Miami number, sir, they've accepted the charges.

Two or three clicks, then a voice, the kind of voice that's still sensual but says it's lived a lot.

– Mr Murchison?

– Speaking.

– Good evening! Nancy Belmont.

– Good evening, Mrs Belmont, I've just found your message on my desk.

– Thank you for calling me back. You saw Glenn just now, didn't you?

– Precisely.

– He's explained the problem and you've agreed to take it on, isn't that right?

– That's quite right. Would you have any further information to give me? I ventured.

– The thing is, Mr Murchison, she said with a moment's hesitation, I think Glenn's underestimating the problem.

– In what way?

– You see, Maria-Liza has never left us for so long without being in touch.

– That's what your husband told me, Mrs Belmont, I replied, quickly switching on to automatic pilot, just in case she was going to dish me up exactly the same story, word for word.

– But Glenn's taking it all lightly, and I'm convinced that Maria-Liza is really in danger.

Surprised, I let go of the switch.

– Could you be more specific? What danger are you talking about, Mrs Belmont?

– Well, Maria-Liza is still a little girl, very pretty and easily influenced . . . .

I fumbled for the 'soaring violins' switch on my

console, but suddenly remembered that Belinda had borrowed it for a friend's engagement party.

– . . . and I realised, quite recently, that she was going around with people she never used to know. Like this singer, Joe de Brown.

– Are you afraid he'll get her to take up singing too, I said, unable to resist the joke.

But Nancy Belmont didn't hear me, or she pretended not to.

– And since she met this boy she's started taking drugs.

I was all ears.

– What kind of drugs, Mrs Belmont?

– I have no idea, but I've noticed it. In the space of a week her behaviour altered. She's always been happy, always smiling, then she started having mood changes for the slightest thing. She would suddenly become sullen, or aggressive, do you know what I mean?

I half understood, since I'd known thousands of girls whose mood was unpredictable; that, though, was without taking any drugs. I hedged.

– Of course. But why are you so sure it's drugs? Have you got any proof?

– No, no, none at all, but I certainly know my little Maria-Liza, and I've read a lot about it. You know it's something that worries nearly all parents these days.

She must have had a subscription to the *Reader's Digest*.

– So you think it's being mixed up with this Joe de Brown that's made her start taking psychotropic drugs?

– I'm sure of it (yes, it was the *Reader's Digest*), and that's why I think she's in danger.

– I understand, Mrs Belmont. What's your opinion

of the relationship between de Brown and Maria-Liza? I asked, already knowing the answer.

– A nothing affair, it won't last.

– Do you get on well with her?

– Of course, Mr Murchison. Maria-Liza has always had everything she wanted, and she's always been a wonderful girl. That's what makes the way she's behaving now so worrying and hard to understand.

I agreed; the picture was getting clearer. Nothing too nasty. Miss femme fatale had taken off into the blue yonder without signalling back to port. But I was quite sure she hadn't forgotten the number of the berth, should the need arise. A little sea trip never did anyone any harm.

– Mrs Belmont, I wound up, I'll be on her trail this very evening. Joe de Brown's band was in New York three days ago. With a bit of luck, he'll still be around. In which case I'll bring you back Maria-Liza, or at the very least I'll put you in touch with her. Don't worry too much. This kind of thing happens every day.

I felt I had reassured her a little. She made me promise once more to give any news to her or her husband as soon as possible. I said I would and hung up.

Night had fallen on the city, and by my reckoning on the rest of the coast too. The neon lights of the hotel next door had come on and were sending me a greenish flash every 3.7 seconds. The problem with neon is that it flickers. Each letter of H.O.T.E.L. lights up singly then they all blaze together for 4.2 seconds before starting all over again for the rest of the night. When you're in a good mood that can put you in a bad one, and when you're in a bad mood it can make you feel like killing somebody. I was still in the former state of mind, and I wasted no time in pulling down the blind so as to spare myself the sight of those bastard lights. That evening I didn't feel like killing.

I went over and opened the door of my fridge, and cracked a bottle of Schlitz. I took the photo of Maria-Liza from my inside pocket and took a good look at it. She was really some looker. I considered her from every angle, then flicked the snapshot over. There were some words written on the back in pencil. Half the letters were missing, but I guessed it must be the photographer's name. Something like Topmer or Toomer, there was no way of telling.

It was getting close to 8 o'clock. I decided to go and freshen up down at the Lone Star, and to use the opportunity for a jaw with Jack about the last band before the desert. Being a barman he was well placed to know.

New York is a town where you have to know your way around. Fact is, although I haven't travelled that much I guess it's the same everywhere. There are joints that have it and joints that don't. Whatever it is, a guy is free to make up his mind. As far as I'm concerned, a little stroll after dark always takes me into bars that are unpretentious, no-nonsense, no three-piece. And believe me, there aren't many of those left. Hence my longstanding affection for the Lone Star, a kind of southern enclave in Manhattan that a good many people regard as the ultimate hangout for New York hicks. But, as I always say, it's better to be a self-respecting hick than a bozo who's too swell-headed to look out of the window to see what the weather's like.

A thin lukewarm drizzle had started coming down, but it didn't really bother me. I like walking in the rain. I especially like the smells of the city, its sounds, feeling its pulse as I stroll along. At those times I feel a bit like the local Tarzan. Around me, the murmur of the jungle, which I know down to its smallest details; and with the wave of a hand I can order eats or hail a taxi. In short, I feel at home.

It was closing on 9 when I walked into the Lone Star, goosing Sally, the girl on the door. I asked her if Jack had come in, and she answered wittily that he must be scouring all the mirror makers in Manhattan Island, cursing me and trying to get the best possible price. True enough, the central mirror of the bar had suffered from our entertainments of the previous night, and it was spangled with giant stars. But for all that, the biggest drinking den in 13th Street wasn't the place to start making like the Milky Way.

With a friendly wave to Frank the barman, who didn't wave back, I headed for a table near the back, cutting between the bar and the stage. A redneck band from down San Antonio way were finishing their sound check as I found my favourite spot, right under a sign proclaiming that 'nobody had ever managed to rape a 38 special'. Settling under this piece of pure Texan humour, I grabbed a menu and an old newspaper that were lying on the next table.

I ordered a chilliburger and a bottle of that first-rate Mexican beer that you drink with lime and salt, like tequila. There were two other tables taken. One by two glum-faced guys in dark suits, who looked as if they were bored or spoiling for a fight. The other by a couple of stray farmers who had probably come along for some country air in the heart of the heartless city. I had a feeling I'd seen one of the suits somewhere before, the one looking really wasted and watching the flies – the guy was next to the kitchen. But after all, wasted-looking types often bear a family resemblance, and I was probably confusing him with some

26

other jerk of that ilk. I skimmed the *Globe* absent-mindedly as I waited for Frank and my chilli, and found some pretty amazing stuff in it. Next year American clairvoyants were predicting the kind of thing that would make your hair stand on end – as a prelude to making it fall out. Besides the Apocalypse, which was galloping closer, easy enough to account for with something arriving on horseback, there was some funny stuff coming our way before too long. For instance, these idiots were pitching the discovery of the mummified body of Hitler in an Arkansas travelling circus, the fall of a giant meterorite in the middle of Peru – which would almost make the earth swerve from its orbit – the gift of speech for cats and dogs through genetic engineering, then the announcement of old Sinatra's candidature for the White House. I was really starting to have fun when Debbie the waitress slid my chilli in front of me, long-faced and without a word. Rather than try and cheer her up with a little repartee, I engaged my burger, which happened to be pretty long-faced too but grilled just the way I like them: carbonised in the flame thrower. I was about to take on a basketful of inoffensive tacos when I felt an unfriendly presence to my left. It was Frank, surveying me, all six feet of him. He kept his distance, but it didn't stop his belly from grazing my arm. A beer gut is a distinguishing mark of quite a few bar owners, so I didn't take it in the slightest as a provocation.

– Topping up? he muttered, with less warmth than a Soviet diplomat.

– I stick to the same gas station, I observed. I'm collecting the stamps.

– You'll need a bundle of them to replace the toy you broke last night, he rejoined, sitting down heavily

on a chair that nonetheless remained impassive.
Didn't your secretary tell you we were closed for
redecoration?

– Come on, Frank, we're not going to smash up a
beautiful friendship for the sake of a mirror. You'll
sleep better if you see less of yourself for a while. And
after all, I've come to pay for the breakages.

His face relaxed a touch. He shoved the remains of
the chewed-up Havana he was holding in his hand
back between his teeth, puffed on it to get it glowing
again and told me:

– 120 dollars, right? Which meant he'd found one
for 70. But I didn't need an argument.

– A day's work, I replied. It's still better than seven
years' bad luck.

– Are you paying tonight?

– Cash!

– Okay! Let's see your wad, he said, almost smiling.

– No problem. And while we're at it, you can let me
have some dope.

– Isn't the booze enough for you any more? he
quipped.

– Listen, Frank, I'm on a case I have to sew up like
yesterday. Have you heard of the Last Chance Band?

His eyes glazed over for a moment, which meant he
was thinking. It didn't last.

– It rings a bell. Hold it, yeah, we had 'em here four
or five months ago. A Washington band, a bit of
everything kinda style. Not bad.

– Can you remember the guys in the band?

– Not much. They were nice enough little fellas.
They didn't exactly invent the four bar, but their stuff
was fine. They had a thing for powdering their noses,
which is bad for the sinuses.

– So you're practising medicine now, or what?

– I keep informed. And I can tell you they had a load of it; they never let up. I even had to tell them to be discreet. I've got my reputation to look out for.

– Did they bring it with them or did they score here?

– Hey, who do you take me for, Sam? Can you see me getting mixed up in coke?

– You'd be able to buy your mirrors wholesale, I quipped.

He took offence.

– I prefer your humour left at home, Sam. No, but the three evenings they played here I noticed that schmuck Tony Gold. You know, the guy who brags about putting the white into White House. When he's around you know the marks aren't far away.

– Have you any idea where I can find this joker?

– Not at the Lone Star any more, that's for sure, if you don't mind. The last time he set foot in here he had to buy a needle and thread to stitch himself up again. But I heard he was hanging out at the Mudd and the Ritz.

– Thanks for the info, I shot at Frank as I slipped quickly towards the exit, and stick the chilli on my slate, I'll drop in again soon.

I could hear him behind me; he was a hair's breadth away from apoplexy, in between two volleys of insults that weren't very flattering to my poor mother. Let it be understood that I'll never allow anyone to utter the slightest word against the woman who had the joy of bringing me into the world, but if you can't forgive your pals a few slip-ups, then who can you forgive?

Between the Mudd and the Ritz I chose the latter, which was just a few blocks from the Lone Star. The streets were virtually deserted, probably because of the rain, even though it was still very light. I ran into a few drunks, and a few joggers, the tough kind, then,

29

crossing over, I noticed that I had the two suits from the café behind me. There was no sure sign that they were following me, but I have a nose for these things. They were neither too close nor too far away, and apparently didn't notice me. I don't like people who don't notice me. When it's apparently, that bugs me even more. But when I got to the door of the Ritz I told myself I'd have time later to check whether those bozos were really tailing me. If they were, they'd be seeing a lot more of me.

I parted with my 10 dollars admission, keeping the ticket stubs to give to Belinda, and went down to the basement to call Joe. By some miracle he was the one to pick up the phone. He quickly lowered his voice when he heard it was me.

– You really want to wipe out my happy home, he began. Are you going in for home wrecking now too?

– Don't worry, I'll rescue you as soon as I've got rid of the tribe of Cheyennes who're riding down my ranch, I laughed, imitating the late lamented Duke. All I need is a little info. You heard of Tony Gold?

– The king of the street dealers?

– That must be him. He deals in coke, doesn't he?

– He deals in everything that brings in the moolah, Joe replied philosophically. But it's true he's fond of coke. Is he bothering you?

– No, I just want the lowdown on him.

– Huh, he's nothin'! He usually gets musicians high. You see him in the clubs all the time. He's a regular one-man band.

– I happen to be calling you from the Ritz, Joe.

– Well, you might run into him. Listen, go to the ground floor bar and ask for Lou from me. If Gold is there, he'll introduce you. Otherwise he'll tell you where you can get hold of him.

– Great. Thanks Joe. Have a nice evening and try to hurry up with your knitting, the nights are still cool.

– Okay, okay. One of these days you'll understand my position. You'll understand, Sam.

– There's no way of telling, but you may be wrong, I reassured him as I hung up.

I went back up to the ground floor, crossing the main room where a youngish crowd was pulsating to the beat of a sound a little less powerful than a helicopter squadron, and reached the bar, where I asked for Lou with the help of my fold-up megaphone. A lucky break – I skipped a whole square on the board – it was him. It looked to me as if he did some moonlighting as a bouncer. He was way over six feet and pulverised five of my fingers when I gave Joe as my introduction. I told him my name and who I was looking for.

– Tony Gold? he bellowed horribly so as to be heard above the neighbouring bombardment. I just saw that little louse not five minutes ago. He went to push his shit to the roadies from the Musculators who were playing just now. I saw him cross the floor just after that; he must have left.

I began to feel the same shadow of demoralisation that must strike every rational being searching for the right form in a maze of bureaucracy. Even as a kid I hated board games. I thanked Lou, using international sign language.

I threaded my way across the room, hurrying down the steps that led to the entrance when, in a flash, I caught sight of the two suits coming through the door with a dubious goosestep. But they were heading for the exit, which must mean they'd already been inside. And since their rocket-style departure was accompanied by piercing screams from the basement, I instinc-

31

tively knew that (1) they weren't following me, (2) they'd relieved themselves in the john without leaving a tip, which was even more serious.

They were scarcely out of sight in the throng of customers waiting in line outside, than the screams redoubled. Without stopping to think, I headed for the floor below and bumped straight into a knot of pre-pubescent girls who were miming terror in a competition for singers. But I quickly realised that they weren't pretending. On the floor, at the back of the little room with its white porcelain fittings, lay a kid of about twenty. At first I thought my two bloodhounds had knocked him out cold, but when I got closer I realised they'd iced him, with a slug right in the middle of his forehead. He was unequivocally dead. And I was unequivocally convinced, without knowing why, that I found the guy I'd been looking for.

FOUR

It was him all right. He'd lived off blow, and it blew him away. As for me, this was a setback before I'd even got ahead. Objectively, it could all have been just a coincidence, an unfortunate combination of circumstances, especially for dead Gold. A settling of scores between suppliers and retailers, or something of the kind; and yet, I was convinced I was involved. The two deadheads following me when I left the Lone Star, and getting to the Ritz before me – it was all too neat. The late Tony must have had something tasty to tell me, but there were big bad wolves who didn't want him to. Had they bumped him off to stop him telling *me* in particular, or to shut him up in general? I had to have the answer to that before anything else. It had all happened by the book. The little pusher had locked himself in one of the booths, and was stashing the green in his shoes. The two killers had come on the scene without any fuss, one of them hanging by the doors while the other – by all accounts the big wasted-looking one – was washing his hands. When Tony had opened the door, the villain with the nice clean hands had grabbed him by the collar and hit him where it hurts then, taking out his piece, had aimed it point blank at the victim's forehead. Nine millimetres. One shot. Fatal. A professional job. Then, with the hysterical screams of the clientele echoing around him, he'd quickly dropped the lifeless body. In ten seconds flat the two evil-doers were in the street, where a dark car – a Buick, according to the doorman – was waiting for them. Routine stuff.

I found myself trapped in the basement, right in the middle of the bovine panic, and I had to wait for the cops from the local precinct to arrive – in no time – on the scene. Statements. Eyewitness accounts. 'Sam Murchison, you again!' The whole shebang.

The red tape wasted most of the night, and I went back to my office to collapse around 2 a.m. I'd had a positive on-the-spot ID-check for Gold, who was already on the records for trafficking and whose shady activities were well known to the police. After two or three whiskies, to the accompaniment of the Hotel Iroquois's perpetual rhythmic flickerings, I sank onto the couch and didn't open my eyes again until around 10, when I was woken by the aroma of Belinda's black coffee. It was a much more humane way of waking up than the day before, but it still made a nice treat for the first physio who came along. One of these days I ought to think about having the springs seen to, or get a new couch, or just drop by my apartment on 17th Street East.

– I can't really see why you insist on renting an apartment, Sam, if you're going to sleep here every night, Belinda aptly observed.

– I need my independence, darling. I have to tend my secret garden.

She shrugged in resignation, opened the blinds that I'd forgotten closing, brought me a mug of steaming

34

coffee on a tray along with the day's papers, and added, laconically:

– I know where you were last night. It's all there in the *Post*.

I'm sure for a lot of people it's lovely to wake up in the morning with their name in the paper. But I prefer to be overlooked.

I was dished up like this: 'Sam Murtchison' (some spelling), 'the famous New York private eye . . . first to be on the scene . . . had spotted the killers just before the drama took place,' etc., etc. The whole thing was under the alluring headline: *Settling of Scores in the Drug Underworld*. The only thing missing was a photo, but they'd forgotten to ask me for one. In any case, if those two icemen were wondering where to find me, they could skip holing up in the country for a week with a pile of phone books. My address appeared in large letters after my name. Some people would call it publicity. I called it dirty. I skipped to the end of the article, took in the name of the hack responsible and asked Belinda to get hold of him right away. I hardly had time to moisten my lips with the coffee when she passed me the phone.

– Randolph Duvall? I asked, checking.

– Speaking.

– Sam Murchison here. MUR-CHI-SON, with no T before the C, and I haven't got a cold. Who allowed you to quote me in your stinking rag?

– You're one of the witnesses cited by the police, Mr Murchison. What's wrong with that?

– What's wrong, asshole, is that I don't tolerate people talking about me without asking me first. You can hide behind whatever you like, the cops, your editor-in-chief, your Scientology, take it, put it all together, and see if I give a damn. And if you have the bad luck to run into me one of these days you'll understand what's made me famous.

I hung up, furious, without leaving the cretin time to stammer out any reply.

– You shouldn't get yourself so worked up Sam, it won't do you any good, Belinda warned me maternally.

– Each to their own, my sweet, I don't like people stepping on my toes, especially when I'm asleep.

While we were on the subject I noticed I'd gone to sleep without even taking the trouble to undress, which isn't hygienic and what's worse, creases your suit. I asked Belinda if she'd seen whether there was a suit back from the cleaners.

– It didn't come back on its own, Sam, and that reminds me, I wanted to let you know that I'm your secretary not your chambermaid.

– We could always consider a promotion, I answered maliciously. Be nice and tell me where you've hidden it, I haven't got time to play hunt the slipper.

– You skunk, she scolded, taking my superb Dixon & Sons charcoal-grey from behind the door along with a clean shirt, a pair of boxer shorts and a pair of socks, all from the Tonkin' Dry Cleaners. If I kept this up I was well on my way to becoming a stockholder in the Chinese laundry business (the one that washes yellower).

As for the case, it wasn't exactly peachy. I'd taken the long way to begin with and now I found myself in a dead end. And the whole thing hadn't brought me a fraction of an inch closer to little Maria-Liza. Besides, I still didn't know whether she was still in Manhattan or not. She was following her band and I had to find out fast where these young talents were if I wanted to get hold of her; so to speak.

I called Belinda back in to ask her advice. Women love being asked for advice; every now and then.

– Tell me, beautiful, if you were handling a little-known rock group and you had to find them a hotel in town, which would you choose?

– Somewhere mid-town, I'd say, she answered with no hesitation. Above the Village and near the clubs. Depending on the budget, I'd go for the Iroquois, next door to the office, the Chelsea or the Gramercy. But the easiest way to find out would be to ask the band's management agency.

Her answer struck me as eminently sensible.

– Good thinking, little one, but why would the management tell us? When people are tracking down showbiz folk in hotels it's usually so that they can bug them. Well, try anyways. Say it's for an interview or something. The Peppermint Lounge office will give you the manager's phone number.

Belinda got busy while I went to immerse myself under an ice-cold shower and put on my suit. I was just rubbing on some aftershave when she knocked on the bathroom door, notebook in hand.

– As a journalist you're pretty lightweight: the band left New York yesterday morning for Montreal. No more band, no more hotel. On the other hand, your case does interest Benett Friedman, the Last Chance Band's manager. He'll let you have an appointment at his office, 222 5th Street, at 3 on the dot. It interests him, but he doesn't seem too impressed.

– Be a pal, find me the hotel they stayed at. I've got a yen to pay a little visit.

Within five minutes this secretary fairy of mine had come up with the goods. It was the Gramercy, on the corner of 21st and Lexington. Yet again, not far from the office. Outside, last night's rain had gone and the weather was grey. I decided to walk to the hotel and have a little breakfast en route so as to dispel the memory of yesterday evening's unhappy chilli.

– I'll call you around 4 or 5, beautiful, I called out to Belinda over my shoulder as I left the office.

After a couple of eggs, a few well-done rashers of ham and three litres of orange juice, I found myself next to the park, opposite the hotel. In New York the area around the Gramcercy is a bit out of the ordinary. A decided flavour of New England predominates, and though you won't exactly find the unemployed there, there isn't that air of ostentatious luxury that really gets on my nerves.

The puny reception guy with the moustache and glasses gave me definite confirmation that the band had left the hotel the previous morning, but he couldn't tell me whether Joe de Brown was with a girl or not.

– There were some girls, but I'm no matchmaker, he ventured to add. On what basis are you asking for this information?

– I'm looking for my sister, and I heard she'd come back here with the musicians after the concert.

– I see, he replied with a broad smile. Listen, I don't really remember. Don't worry. A young girl who follows musicians after a concert usually knows what she's up to. In any case I can assure you none of them is with us any longer.

I told myself she must have stayed at the Gramercy. According to her father she'd been seen at the corner of 21st and Third, in other words one block away. All the same, to double check I took out the photo of Maria-Liza and put it under the receptionist's nose. I might as well have offered him a cigarette. He didn't smoke. I concluded that he needed either to change

38

his glasses or his job. A large part of a hotel's reputation depends on the good humour of these flunkies and their memory for faces. I gave him the benefit of these opinions and he only half appreciated them.

I was spitting distance from the Gramercy bar, so I went in there to have another coffee and a smoke. I tried to pump the barman, but it was useless. This meant I had no proof that Maria-Liza had been in the hotel, and I'd done a lot of walking for nothing. It was only 11.30 and I found myself with time to kill again before my appointment with Friedman. This is a job where patience counts big time.

I went back into the lobby, giving my pal on reception a meaningful glance, and made a call to Harry Marotta, an inspector in the New York 10th Bureau. I'd met Marotta during my time in the Bronx. We used to be teamed up together sometimes, and he was just about the only okay guy in the bunch. He wasn't stingy when it came to handing out ammunition, but he always kept an eye on things, and he wasn't one of those trigger-happy psychopaths who confuse the street with a rifle range. He was one of the few who understood that in everyday life the targets are alive and not necessarily guilty. At the same time he never shied away from trouble, and he couldn't wait until his adversary had emptied three rounds at him before returning fire. All this, along with the fact that he could shoot the top off a bottle at fifty yards with hardly a notch on the glass, had carved him out a rock-solid reputation that not many crooks would take on. I'd always kept in touch with Harry. He'd got me out of quite a few bureaucratic jams, and in return I'd tipped him off occasionally. I asked him if he had a minute to have a bite with me, and we arranged to meet at the Italian on the corner of Bleeker and Sixth. I stayed a little longer in the Gramercy bar, leafing through their copy of the *Post*, which was like balm to my heart, since there were still a few pages where I wasn't mentioned. Half an hour later I leapt into a taxi and had it drop me outside the restaurant.

Harry had just arrived and was waiting for me at the bar, sipping a beer.

– The man whose name is on everyone's lips, he announced, pumping my hand.

– I want everybody to cool it, I replied in a stage voice meant for the whole room, which consisted of around 98.5 per cent cops – the Italian luncheonette was for the most part the local copshop's canteen. Right now the star of the show is having lunch.

– The star of the show must have a few little things to ask me, Harry chortled, waving me to sit down opposite him.

– You see right through me, I said. How's your family, and can I have pasta with meat sauce and a Rolling Rock?

– It's growing, Loretta is expecting her seventh, he replied, before yelling my order. Thanks for asking.

– You know, I told him, they've just invented something that works very well for women. It's the size of a pearl, you swallow it, and it stops you from conceiving without making you sterile.

– Don't joke about these things, Sam, you know I don't like it.

We put ourselves on ice while we polished off our pasta, which, by contrast, was fresh not frozen.

– Have you heard of Tony Gold? I slipped in between mouthfuls.

– Now we have it, he gloated. Next time make sure you don't threaten a journalist, they can't stand that, Sam.

40

– I see word gets round fast. But all the same you're not going to hold it against me for warning him off.

– It was Hopper, the young guy who's handling the case, who got a call this morning from this kid at the *Post*. He didn't seem at all happy.

– I couldn't give a damn. And it's not nice to tell tales. Anyway, the next time he'll think twice about what he writes, it'll help him do his job better. Well, what about Tony Gold?

– It's not my business, I don't know what you had against him, but you could have chosen better. We were keeping tabs on him, but there are bigger fish around at the moment. And this kind of score settling on the drug scene happens practically every day. As long as they're only shooting each other we keep to the side lines. Just think that the estimated number of junkies in New York alone is two hundred thousand. Before coming here to see you I looked up the computer and took down some figures that'll cheer you up. Leaving drug users out of it – he went on, taking a card out of his pocket – for yesterday alone we came up with this: five bank jobs, two hundred and fifty aggravated robberies, nineteen rapes, four hundred and sixty burglaries, and two hundred and forty-eight armed assaults. A total of one thousand six hundred and twenty-five crimes overall, and eight hundred and seventy misdemeanours. In connection with these, we arrested twelve suspects for homicide, made sixty-one collars for theft, four for rape, thirty-eight for burglary and fifteen for armed assault.

– I'm dying laughing, I told him. But statistics won't solve my problem. I've the nasty impression that this is something more than a feud, Harry. I'm convinced that the two gunmen who blew away Gold were

41

following me when I got to the Ritz and wanted to stop him talking to me.

– And he'd have squealed on other suppliers who in turn would have squealed too. Enough to fill the Brooklyn phone book. Believe me, Sam, there's a lot of charlie in circulation here. You can step on one ant, but not the anthill.

– Nice, I acknowledged. If you happen to find out any more, could you let me know?

– If you like, but take my word for it, you're going nowhere with this.

We stayed at his Iti haunt for an hour or so, shooting the breeze. He told me the joke about the Poles stuck all night on an escalator because of a power cut, and other equally edifying things, then, after one last espresso, we went our separate ways.

I hung around the Village for a while, then made up my mind to take the subway up to 57th Street. I dived on to the express and found I had a whole compartment to myself. At the far end a tramp was quietly sleeping it off, oblivious of the headlong rattle of the train. There I was, waiting for my stop, when through the connecting doors what should I see but a face I knew from somewhere, even if I didn't quite recognise it. When he was about twenty yards away, creeping towards me, I ID'd Mr Wasted, followed close behind by his pal. From what I could tell they didn't know that I'd noticed them because they were making a great play of sneaking up on me. As they were about to come through the connecting doors, I leapt behind my seat and pulled my gun. This way I managed to avoid a bullet that shattered the glass I'd been leaning against seconds before. Metal calls for metal, and I lost no time sending them three samples from my collection, but they seemed to know them already, because they sent them straight back at me. The racket some-how failed to wake up the drunk, though that ceased to matter when a bullet lodged in his left cheek at the end of a treacherous ricochet. They must have had an M16 flown in in the meantime; they were sweeping the place with non-stop fire in a way that made it impossible for me to move. The subway was rattling away on all cylinders and I could see the signs for 31st, 32nd and 33rd Streets going past. I had to hold out until 42nd and Grand Central, but I guessed with nothing giving they'd turn off the sprinklers. And I guessed right. There was a split second of calm that Wasted-Face used to move into the compartment, pointing an elegant 44 Magnum in my direction. His considerable girth was no drawback to suppleness and speed. Maybe supple enough, but certainly not speedy enough to dodge the little present I fired straight into his skull. The bullethole made a nice crater to let the air in, air the guy abruptly stopped breathing. He fell flat, backwards, heavily. He no longer had any expression on his face, but this way now he was really wasted.

From his buddy's end there was no comparative silence, which I didn't fully have time to enjoy as the screeching of brakes drowned out the rumbling of the train. 'The train of death', as the airhead from the *Post* would inevitably write, entered the station. And believe me the platform wasn't empty. About two and a half thousand potential victims had chosen that very line to take them uptown. Head down, I considered what moves wasted guy 2 might make, but as soon as the train came to a halt I saw him diving right into the crowd, elbowing everybody out of the way, like a quarterback running with the ball. In two seconds flat he had cut through the three-deep bank of passengers and vanished up the stairs. I had no hope of catching him. I swiftly stashed my weapon and, cool as a cucumber, left the devastated compartment as if I was leaving Radio City Hall on a gala night. I was quickening my step when the hue and cry started behind me, but I didn't turn back, using the crowd to get me out into the open air.

It was obvious I could be pretty certain now that Tony Gold owed his one-way ticket to me. And that's how I started out in search of a runaway heiress and ended up on one of the murkiest cases in my career. And that's saying something!

FIVE

It took me a few seconds to check there was nobody waiting for me outside the subway. All the same, I kept checking that Wasted-Face's buddy wasn't anywhere in the vicinity as I walked the ten blocks to Friedman's office. I was a little early for my appointment and I treated myself to a pause in the nearest bar to take my bearings and sink a beer.

The Last Chance Band was mixed up in something pretty heavy. And I was convinced now that little Maria-Liza wasn't very far from the eye of the cyclone. It had started with one of the band's suppliers being rubbed out, then efforts focussed more directly on me. Someone obviously wanted to stop me getting near the band, and maybe near Maria-Liza. What they didn't know was that this was precisely the way to make me determined to find them. But why didn't this broad get in touch with her folks? Was she being held prisoner or what? There wasn't much I knew. But I love finding out.

At bang on 3 I found myself on the landing of the eighteenth floor where the offices of World Talent Agency – Benett Friedman Management – had its home. I underlined the point by banging three times

45

on the door, eliciting an invitation to come in in a gooey female voice. It was no surprise to find a secretary inside – a chick who was emphatically brunette, with a hairdo that must have been tortured into shape. After asking me for my name and the purpose of my visit, inspecting my card and okaying everything, she proposed that I take a seat in an ample leather armchair while I waited for her boss to see me. She was even courteous enough to inform the aforementioned boss that I was there. He told her he'd be free in a few moments. I expressed an encouraging wink in this female warder's direction, and she answered me with a lopsided smile exposing an even row of teeth that were much too white and a huge wad of chewing gum. I lit a Winston and looked around the room, which was plastered with dozens of gold discs. To all appearances Friedman had a solid stable, if the names of the artistes inscribed under the discs were anything to go by. And he was no newcomer either, because I recognised his name on one of the plaques engraved in '72. His secretary had gone back to tapping away nervously on her Remington meanwhile, chewing her gum with a degree of vulgarity that didn't bother me at all. Muffled music came from the end of the corridor that opened out on the right. I lifted one of the newspapers spread out on the low table beside the armchair and started leafing through it. It was a music industry trade. So and so had sold three million platters, the record industry was gradually getting back on its feet, the video promo was reinvigorating business, rockabilly was making a comeback, all in all the kind of stuff I can't get enough of.

I glanced at my watch and saw it was already nearly 3.06. And if there's one thing in life that annoys me, it's being kept waiting. I put down my *Billboard* and addressed myself to Miss Hairdo:

– Maybe he's dropped off?

– I beg your pardon?

– I said, maybe Mr Friedman's dropped off.

– He'll be with you in a few moments. Can I get you a coffee?

– With pleasure, black and no sugar if that's all right with you.

She got up, looking less than delighted, and stepped out into the corridor to make with the filter. It was 3.10 when she returned with my beverage, carrying it with care but without sugar.

– If you have a moment, I can take you to see the uncut version of *Gone With The Wind* while we wait for Mr Friedman to wake up, I wisecracked after thanking her.

– Be patient, Mr Murchison, she answered unsmiling, Mr Friedman is a very busy man.

– No problem, I replied, I've got the rest of the year in front of me.

It was obvious she wasn't paid to laugh. She sat down again behind her typewriter, ignoring me completely. I finished my butt as I drank the dishwater she'd brought me, and to pass the time I decided to make some holes in the armrest of the chair with it. I have no patience. It's my biggest defect.

Around 3.13, my hostess looked up from her dismal typing and started sniffing.

– I can smell burning, she announced unerringly.

– If you ask me, he's fallen asleep smoking, I said to scare her.

She was getting up to locate the source of the fire when the intercom started talking:

– Show Mr Murphinson in, Miss Smolen.

47

I slid what was left of the cigarette behind the cushion of the armchair and went over to the brunette's desk. Looking around anxiously, she invited me to follow her into the corridor, knocked discreetly on the second door to the left and showed me in.

I found myself in a flashily furnished office a little smaller than the lobby of the Empire State Building. The decor was unobtrusive: little bits of wall sandwiched between gold, even platinum discs. I sank up to my knees into a carpet that was awfully reminiscent of a wheatfield before the harvest – and there sure was plenty of bread here. At the far end, with his back to the window, the aforementioned Friedman lolled slumped in an armchair rocker with his feet on the desk. I took an immediate dislike to him.

He was dry and oily in equal parts, squeezed into a sleeveless waistcoat. Topping a face that looked around the forty mark was a pate of emphatic baldness. A decidedly hooked nose and large unamazed eyes surmounted a mouth whose lips had no contours. If he was after the *Playgirl* centrefold he'd have to shell out for the privilege.

The only spark of life to be seen in this façade was in his bright, sharp eyes, which fastened onto me insistently like they were taking soundings. Without even bothering to get up or apologise for keeping me waiting, he asked me to come down to his level, which meant an armchair across the desk from him. I preferred to remain on my feet.

– I'm sorry I'm a little ahead of time, I said sarcastically.

Friedman ignored this and made no move to get up.

– Well Mr Murphinson, I gather you're interested in one of my bands.

– MUR-CHI-SON, not Murphinson, I corrected,

irritated. And I'm only indirectly interested in your protegés, Mr Fritzman.

– Friedman. And for what reason, might I know, is a P.I. even indirectly interested in the Last Chance Band? Or is it your private nose you're sticking in here?

He was some joker. If he kept it up, there'd be one nose I'd sure stick one on, and it was his.

– I see I'm dealing with a wit, I retorted, still waiting for the wisdom. And I'm pleased about that. Would you believe I'm looking for a young girl who's been seduced by one of your rising stars: Maria-Liza Belmont; she's granting her favours to Joe de Brown. Have you heard about this?

– Of course, Mr Murchison, I know about every little thing my artists do.

It seemed obvious that he kept track of every single dollar that went through his employees' hands. And his 'artists', the way he put it, were nothing but hired hands.

– Then you can tell me where I can find the Belmont girl. Her parents are anxious to speak to her and she hasn't been in touch since she met de Brown.

– Well, it was my impression that it was just a fling, he answered. Unfortunately, my professional competence only stretches to looking after my bands. I don't put in overtime as a chaperone.

I began to see red.

– Listen, Friedman, your professional competence, such as it is, likewise your employees and your overtime, all mean as much to me as the chocolate discs hanging around this room. I'm asking you where the Belmont girl is, full stop.

– My dear Mr Murchison, I can understand your anxiety. You have a job to do and that's only reasonable. All I can tell you is that the Last Chance Band left New York yesterday morning for Montreal, where they were playing last night, and that right now they must be on the Montreal-Paris flight.

– You mean to say they've left for Europe with the kid? I asked, disconcerted.

– Paris is in fact in Europe and the Belmont girl with Joe de Brown. You see, there's not much you can do.

I thought I detected a gleam of satisfaction in his eyes.

– I can always take a plane, it's catching on nowadays.

Friedman showed a flicker of unease.

– Let me tell you something, Murchison, he went on, a rock group is a fragile thing. At the moment de Brown is infatuated with a little girl and if you interfere and take her away from him it's the whole band you'll be jeopardising. I've told you where they were, I'll give you the number of the hotel in Paris, but you're going to leave them alone. Do you understand me?

He grabbed a pen and, after looking up one of his card indexes, scribbled out a name and number that he handed to me. I didn't thank him. I came straight back at him.

– Tell me, Friedman, have you heard about any business with drugs in the fragile balance of your band?

– What does that have to do with your inquiry, he asked me tersely.

– You don't need to know, I told him, to put him at his ease. Have you heard, or haven't you?

– It isn't something I would discuss with you, he declared. I've given you your information, there's nothing else that concerns you.

This really needled me. I reached towards him, grabbed him by the lapels and jerked his stupid ugly mug close to my own much prettier one.

– On the contrary it interests me a hell of a lot and you're going to tell me everything you know, creep.

Friedman lost his cool, stammered into the void and talked.

– Calm down, Murchison, all I meant to say was that these things have to be kept a bit quiet, know what I mean?

– Of course, I assented, but I'm an exception, huh?

I relaxed my grip and dropped him back into his armchair. He pulled himself together pathetically.

– There are always drugs around. But as far as I know, the kids in the Last Chance don't go too far.

– Have you ever heard of Tony Gold?

He answered in the negative, pretty well convincingly.

– Never, is he a new musician?

– That's right, I confirmed, but you should get a move on to sign him up, it doesn't do to let talent get cold.

I turned and made for the door, hacking my way through the weeds. As I went out, I called to him:

– We're bound to meet again Benett, don't forget me.

I slammed the door and headed down the corridor, passing Miss Smolen arguing with a fire extinguisher beside my old armchair. She was in a rage, but she didn't have time to turn round when I told her it was well done. I went back down the eighteen floors and back into the same bar as before, somewhat perplexed.

I treated myself to a few large whiskies and dug a ten-cent piece out of my pocket to call Belinda. I was

51

very surprised when I got no answer. I tried the number again to make sure. She'd probably gone out to buy one of those little items women often find they have to have, especially right in the middle of the afternoon.

I rang Harry's number at the precinct, and was lucky to find him not out on a case.

– You'd think I was becoming indispensable, he cracked.

– I'm ringing you from around Grand Central, I lied. You'd think they'd found oil deposits underground, there's so much action in the neighbourhood.

– It was underground, but it wasn't oil, he remarked wittily enough. More like cold meat.

– Somebody I'd know? I asked.

– Let's say he wasn't an unknown, at any rate in your case. Tommy O'Malley, professional gunslinger. And then there's an old soak, still unidentified.

– Tommy O'Malley? But that's the guy who knocked off Tony Gold! You should be delighted, the statistics are evening things out.

– Hey there! he let out softly, in the first place how do you know . . . ?

– Self-defence, old pal, have your ballistics people check it out, and thanks for the name.

– Sam . . . .

I hung up abruptly, leaving him on a cliffhanger, which would give us plenty to talk about the next time. I had another try at reaching my office, but drew a blank again. I made up my mind to go down there. I paid for my Wild Turkeys, went out onto the sidewalk and hailed a taxi as I lit a cigarette. I gave the cabbie my address and realised at once that I'd come across Manhattan's most garrulous. To cap it all, he couldn't stand smoke. It must have stopped him breathing between sentences. I lowered the window a little just as the radio was doing a commercial for Smucker's jam. He picked up on the commercial for starters:

– You know who used to make good jam? he asked me.

I didn't answer, but he wasn't waiting for an answer.

– Ashford & Peters. That was real jam. With the cherry, you'd get whole cherries in the pot.

I made a show of looking at the buildings we passed, as we went back down towards Times Square along Broadway, with a few more bumps than a canoe closing in on Niagara Falls.

– In those days you could still enjoy driving in New York, but now it's finito. The holes in the roads are so big you could disappear in them, you and your car, and nobody'd notice.

I thought to myself that after I'd got out this was the best thing that could happen to him. I've always been physically repelled by all the retards who spoil life by telling you how much better things used to be.

That didn't stop him from going on.

– I bet it would cost them millions to fill up all the holes and repair the roads in this damned city. And that won't happen so long as we've got those deadloss politicians that call themselves liberals in the town hall.

He was ragging North–South relations when we reached the corner of my street. Still without a word, I paid the fare and left him a tip that would buy him some peanuts to fill the holes in his head. I went into my building and up fast, as fast as my elevator at least, which is approaching the status of a historic monument. I was surprised to find the door of the office left ajar, not the sort of thing Belinda would do.

53

Nor did she go in for tying herself to a chair, gagged and in a state of semi-consciousness with her blouse in shreds and six or seven ugly cigarette burns on her bazooms. I concluded somebody must have helped her, as well as turning over all the files, the furniture and just about everything that was usually the other way up. The poor darling had fainted, but she was alive. Taking care, I untied her and went to dampen a towel with cold water, then patted it gently on her face to make her come round.

– Sam, she said recognising me, with a grimace of pain, oh Sam! It's terrible.

– There now, I comforted her, it's over little dove. You been having a party here or what? This didn't even raise a smile from her, but I didn't mind. Realising she was half naked, she quickly covered herself.

– At least there's no question they're real now, I said.

– It hurts, Sam. My God, it was horrible. There were three of them. They all came at me at once. They slapped me. They ransacked the whole place yelling and breaking everything. They did . . . that, she gasped, indicating her assets.

– Calm down, Belinda, calm down. Who came here and why?

– I don't know, she replied breathlessly, I've never seen them before. Three men who were very strong, very evil. One of them had a crazy look in his eyes. I thought he was going to kill me. I couldn't see their faces, they'd covered them with scarves. My God! They were looking for the file on Liza Belmont, and though I swore to them there was no file, they wouldn't believe me. Look what they've done. Oh, it hurts, Sam.

It certainly wasn't a pretty sight. Neither Belinda

nor the office. I've never been obsessed with tidiness, but this was taking things too far.

– Sam, she went on, they told me to warn you that if you don't drop this case they'll come back and set fire to the office, with me inside.

Threats? Those goons dared to threaten you?

There's nothing I hate more than threats. Especially when they're indirect.

– Okay Belinda. Take my doc's number, go home and ask him to come and make you better. Just rest and wait for my call. Don't come back here before I tell you to. Promise?

She had no trouble promising. I slipped her two 10 dollar bills and told her to take a cab. It wasn't a good day for the subway. I helped her up, draped her coat around her shoulders, and handed her her purse after I'd picked up its contents off the floor. I was surprised to find my photograph sticking out of her wallet. She was a good kid. I went with her out to the landing and after she'd persuaded me she'd be okay, I put her in the elevator before going back to the battlefield.

Those bastards had really turned the place over. Even down to my bottle of Jack Daniels, which they'd had the bright idea of smashing against the wall. I tidied up a bit, hurriedly, putting most effort into setting the desk, chairs, armchair and sofa upright. Luckily they hadn't ripped out the phone. Probably an oversight.

I was mad as hell and I think if I'd had one of them in my hands at that moment I'd have invited my shareholders from the Tonkin' to cut him up fine.

SIX

It was 5.30 by the time I opened my eyes; I was horizontal on my sofa. I must have dropped off for a while – I find it's the best way of unwinding. Dozing, I'd forgotten the wasteland that greeted me again like a bad dream. My rage returned at once, unabated, and I got down to gathering up the hundreds of papers that were scattered all around, putting the card indexes back together and replacing the drawers of the filing cabinet. All this took me a good half hour, and then when I felt like rewarding my hard work with a little shot of Jack, I remembered that the last bottle had varnished one of the walls. I checked the fridge, behind the curtain next to the shower area – miraculously untouched – but it was as empty as the inside of Dan Quayle's skull. I lit up. The office had regained a semblance of life and I made use of the onslaught to fill a garbage bag brimful with old kack.

With this I went down to the street, got rid of the trash and headed for the nearest corner store to stock up. I bought a couple dozen cans of Schlitz, Miller and Rolling Rock, cigarettes, honey roast almonds, the late edition of the *Post*, and two imperial quarts of Jack Daniels. On the way, I also got a dozen shot glasses and a new coffee machine, since nothing had survived the hurricane. Finally I dropped in to the cleaners to pick up three shirts, and promised I'd soon be sending them a cargo of new merchandise.

When I got back to the office I felt much better. I took my second shower of the day, rubbed on some toilet water, put on an immaculate shirt, opened a frosty Schlitz, and, nibbling on some almonds, began making the inventory of damages, to be sent to Belmont.

I'd got to around 164 dollars when it occurred to me to give Belinda a call. She'd got home okay and admitted she was still shaky. The doc had prescribed a miracle ointment that had relieved the pain quickly. He had also assured her the scars would be gone in a few weeks. That had calmed her down a bit.

I explained where I'd got to with the case: the gunfight in the subway, the interview with Friedman, and the band's departure for France. I promised I'd keep her up to date and repeated my ban on her setting foot here without my authorisation. She didn't need telling twice.

– Oh, Sam, with all this I completely forgot to tell you that Sergeant Muldaur called. In fact he told me it was one of your bullets that had shattered O'Malley's skull. He's very concerned and he wants to talk to you about it.

– Be nice, Belinda, tell him I've left all my ammunition with the pawnbroker to pay my utilities. And if he's really concerned he can find out from Harry Marotta.

I left a message at Belmont's hotel since, naturally, he'd gone out, then I picked up the *Post*. 'The train of death' – it was in these very words that those clowns described the subway episode. 'Another revenge killing in the middle of New York. An innocent victim in the killer's crossfire. Traffic brought to a halt for seventeen minutes. Growing insecurity in Manhattan.' Followed by the usual hogwash. But for once I wasn't bold-type; my name wasn't even mentioned. And I enjoyed picturing what Randolph Duvall's face would have looked like if he'd even brought up my first name in another article. He would have had plenty of time to open the debate between freedom of information and plastic surgery. A great debate, natch.

I called Joe before he left his office, told him the score, and asked him to do me a favour and put me in touch with people who'd known O'Malley. He understood the problem perfectly, appreciated how important it was and agreed to come and have dinner with me to talk it over. On one condition: I didn't breathe a word to Ruth, which seemed reasonable.

Night was falling gently on New York and, lighting another cigarette, I settled comfortably into my old armchair. The Iroquois would soon be renewing its distress signals, futile as they were, since it was nearly always empty. A few police sirens in the distance were gathering next morning's news stories for the *Post* and the next door building site work had just stopped, as if by magic. I slurped my Schlitz, savouring these few moments of relative calm, when the telephone's peremptory ring pulled me out of the vague torpor that was beginning to take over. I lifted the receiver.

– Mr Murchison, please.

– Speaking.

– Please hold, I've got Mr Belmont for you.

I waited through three clicks, then Belmont came on the line. He seemed in a hurry.

– You called me, Murchison?

– As we agreed, sir. I've located your daughter, but the case seems a lot more complicated than I thought.

– What do you mean? he said anxiously. Have you seen her?

I summarised the situation, sparing him the worst details, but still impressing upon him that this wasn't just a straightforward case of runaway lovers. He hassled me with questions which I mostly avoided. This made him want to know more and gave him the impression that I wasn't telling him everything.

– I'm very worried, Mr Murchison. What you're saying is that Maria-Liza has left for Europe with this Joe de Brown, that persons unknown have made it clear to you that they wanted to be left alone, even going as far as ransacking your office, but you believe there's more to it. Is that it?

– It's one way of looking at it. The question is: do you want me to go any further with this, or will the number of the hotel in Paris be enough? Maybe you can speak to her tomorrow morning?

I gave him the number.

– I need to think it over, Mr Murchison, and discuss it with my wife. How can I get hold of you again, let's say tomorrow morning?

I gave him Belinda's home number.

– Ring this number. I'll be sure to get any messages.

With a repeated assurance that he'd get back to me next morning with an answer, he hung up. He seemed less pressed for time and more upset. He had no idea what a dirty business his kid was mixed up in.

So I had time on my hands that evening to try and find the guys who'd come to my office for some twisto hijinx. Or at least try to establish their whereabouts. But to do this I needed Joe's help. He knocked on my door a little before 7, completely recovered from our jamboree two days before.

– I feel like I'm cheating on my wife when I come here, he told me, kind of delighted with this idea.

– Watch out, don't get the wrong idea, Joe, my heart is no longer my own, I told him warningly.

– Ruth claims you're an evil spirit incarnate, out to turn me off the straight and narrow.

– It's the first time I've heard that 'two bourbons' was an incantation to Satan, I said, aiming to reassure him. But forget her for a little while. Everything's okay, relax, I said as I poured him a stiff one.

– Sure thing, he agreed, so laid back it was almost worrying. (Then he caught up with me.) So you've got problems?

– Nothing too serious. As I was telling you, I've had somebody try to blow me away, I've been threatened and I've had my office used for combat manoeuvres with my secretary practically raped. Otherwise, everything's fine, and the dentist you recommended has done miracles.

– Sam, I've the impression the guys you're dealing with aren't kidding. Watch out. I think I'm right in saying this is a highly organised gang. Later on we'll drop in on some contacts who're bound to be able to put us in the picture. On one condition: promise me there'll be no rough stuff.

– I swear, Your Honour, I answered, raising my right hand.

– I'm asking you for my own sake, Sam. I have connections with a lot of people and in set-ups like this I'm the one vouching for you, know what I mean?

– Perfectly, there's nothing to worry about.

– Otherwise, I suggest we go and have a bite to eat

before getting down to business. I haven't eaten all day and I'm starved. Any objection?

– None, Your Honour.

– Then I'll take you to a Thai place I discovered last week on the edge of Chinatown. Okay?

– Great, for once I'm being spared your old Vietnamese.

We poured ourselves another shot of JD, while concurring on the reliable quality of the product and agreeing that every right-thinking man should clock up a visit to the Lynchburg distilleries in Tennessee at least once in his life. We promised ourselves to get along there as soon as we had a few days off and, Joe agreed, without Ruth.

We reached Chinatown around 8, when it was really buzzing with life. The stores hadn't closed yet and business was just getting going in the restaurants. Ours was in Bayard Street, almost opposite the Criminal Court, which brought back some bad memories for Joe. He'd been a guest there for several months in his early days, through shady dealing in registration plates.

– Believe me, he insisted, the grass ain't greener on the other side.

I had no trouble taking his word for it, so he was spared another sentence. He was pleased about that.

Joe had been quite right. This restaurant was a real find, and we stuffed ourselves unstintingly with pork satays, octopus salad, grilled perch with a ginger sauce, and Thai noodles, the whole thing washed down with a local light beer, ice cold. It was an unpretentious little joint, the way I like them, as is often the case in Chinatown. But the chow was first class. Joe was in top form. Business was good and I took good care not to inquire too closely about the details. In any case, he was gloating over having dumped a competitor 'in the shit' – a guy who'd been a bit too greedy with his profit margins. Next thing the guy had tried to bring Joe down, but it had really hurt him. A deadbeat, was Joe's verdict.

This dinner had boosted our morale. And, after a few beers, Joe had slightly modified his stand on the question of what was a no-no when it came to rough stuff with his pals.

– Sam, he told me, you're my buddy. You're even my only real buddy. And whoever those sons of bitches who've been giving you a hard time for the last couple of days are, I can't let them off the hook. If I ever run into them, believe me, the two of us'll make them behave.

This was the Joe I loved. Not the guy who'd gone soft under the influence of a 'better' half who made him get a mortgage and that bullshit. Now that he was with me he was escaping her influence like a rocket out of orbit. It came down to him switching poles of attraction. I confided this insight.

We paid our bill. The streets had emptied since 8. People were having dinner now and only a few hurrying shadows nipped along the deserted alleyways. It has to be said that Chinatown isn't the safest part of the world after dark.

To get back to my story, Joe had decided the best thing to do was take ourselves down a particular alley that joins Broadway and Seventh Avenue, between 47th and 48th Streets. The Fascination Video Arcade was a kind of electronic amusement arcade that ran the length of it and was used as a meeting place by a lot of local lowlife, the kind that always have plenty of hot dope to impart. We got there in his old Chevrolet, which he'd brought to pick me up at the office. Joe had always preferred to have used cars 'which are less conspicuous if need be'. 'Always best to have a used car for discretion,' I would always retort. It made us laugh. But it doesn't take much to make Joe and me laugh. He forewarned me:

– These aren't big fish we're going to meet, but they're usually hip to just about everything.

– The cops must keep it staked out if they meet there a lot, I surmised.

– It's not really a meeting place, he told me. More like a hangout. There's two exits and plenty of side doors.

– It's like the jungle, I orated, highly struck by this colourful image. The wild beasts meeting at the watering hole.

– The gentleman is succumbing to cliché, he pointed out, quite rightly, but don't worry, nothing ever goes down there. They've got the mid-town north district of the Anti Crime Union that's never off their back. But they only ever catch small fry. The other day one of the Union leaders was telling me: 'We put them inside, and it has as much effect on them as the death of their great-grandmother. It's like a rest period in their business life. They take a few days' vacation and come out again as if nothing had happened. It seemed to get him down. Hey, look, he said, pointing out the window.

We were reaching the 'Arcade of Crime', as Duvall would one day say of it, and Joe was drawing my attention to a cab parked further ahead, fifty yards from the entrance.

– That's Sullivan and MacFerlow, police officer and sergeant respectively. They spend the night here, waiting for a break, with their infra-red binoculars. When the bait's good, something bites.

Joe slowed down alongside them, hooted discreetly and gave them a respectful salute. The one behind the wheel answered with a small gesture that much more likely meant go and fuck yourself than 'it's you – what-a-surprise-but-where've-you've-been-all-this-time?'

– Where've they been brought up? Joe wondered.

– They're not rude enough to be bad guys, I assured him.

Joe parked his antique in 47th Street and we walked the half block to the arcade. The clientele came down to a score or so of odd types, all very busy manhandling their machines: Super-Cobra, Robotron, Alpine Ski, Jungle King, Bag Man and other Pac-Man games, in the midst of an infernal din of gurgles, roars, groans, beeps, gunfire, explosions, twittering and screeching. Stuff that wears down your nerves. Nobody was paying any attention to us.

– I didn't know these games were legal for people over eighteen, I yelled in Joe's ear.

The average age was more like twenty-five or twenty-six.

– Wait here, he told me, and headed towards a door, probably a concealed exit, given the feel of the place.

I gave the customers the once-over, and lit a cigarette. The customers were kind of edgy. They were yelling and shouting, they were kicking the machines and letting out screams to go with the volleys of gunfire. Not the ideal spot to unwind in. Joe was back right away, signalling me to follow him.

– We're in luck tonight, he murmured.

We went down a corridor in pitch darkness that led us outside to a dead end where a white convertible Rolls was parked with its lights out, facing the alley's exit. The rear door opened automatically and Joe beckoned me to join him inside. A voice emanating from a huge silhouette that was seated some yards away told us to sit down opposite one another, and we did so as the door was closed.

– Sam, allow me to introduce the king of the gypsies. My friend, Sam Murchison, Joe said, gesturing towards me.

The silhouette touched a button on the partition to his right and a dim light illuminated the car's interior.

– Delighted, Mr Murchison. The greeting came from a fat lady massively swathed in white sable – she seemed to belong to the male sex, though.

– The pleasure is mine, I affirmed, with the respect due to royalty.

– Thank you. How can I be of service to you?

His Highness was in full regalia. Broad gold rings dangled from his ears. His front teeth weren't dangling, but they were made of the same metal, and, as a finishing touch, a thin moustache was etched above his thick upper lip. I spared him the full-length version of my story and only divulged the trailer, with O'Malley in the leading role.

– I know all about O'Malley already, and I even know that you were his adversary in this duel to the death, he announced pompously. Congratulations, by the way, O'Malley was known to be one of the best shots in New York.

I bowed.

– All I can tell you, without giving away any secrets . . . (and without risking your own health, I added to myself) is that O'Malley and his associate, the one your bullet missed, were working, how shall we say, in the area of import-export consortiums. Columbian and Bolivian products, if you get my meaning.

– I get it.

– So that's where I'd advise you to direct your inquiries.

– Another thing, while I was out I had a visit at my office from three demolition experts insisting that I drop the case I'm working on at the moment.

– I'd be thinking it's the same crew, he declared. Which, I can promise you with no hesitation, has zero to do with me.

– Naturally. Can't you be any more precise? I asked, knowing it was pointless.

– I've made it clear. This is all I can do as a courtesy out of regard for our mutual friend, Joe Mangelson, in present company.

I glanced questioningly at Joe Mangelson, in present company, to see if it would really be *lèse-majesté* to tan this dodo's hide so as to make him more talkative. In any case I've never been much of a monarchist. He saw at once where I was heading, and spoke up.

– My friend Sam and I are immensely grateful for this precious information, he said. Don't think twice about asking me to return the favour should the need arise.

– I won't, Joe, the gypsy turned king assured him, as the door opened again with the same automatic movement.

I took my leave of His Greatness, stooped to get out and found the car surrounded by four softshoe gorillas who'd come out of nowhere. Joe passed in front of me, delivered another thank you, thoughtfully greeted the bodyguard and dragged me towards the Arcade along the same corridor.

– Not very chatty, your king.

– Wise up, he wised me up, he told you plenty. You

66

were hardly expecting him to give you names and addresses, were you?

– That's true, I agreed. What's this clown's line? Foxhunting or holy wars?

– A bit of everything, a big pile of the big H goes through his hands here.

– I see, I wisecracked, my kingdom for a Horse.

– You'll never change, observed Joe.

Once we were inside the Arcade, his advice was to leave things be.

– I know you'd love to get hold of one of your visitors, but it looks like you've stumbled on something big. You might be better off dropping the whole thing.

– No way, brother, when somebody breaks one of my teeth I bust his jaw, you know me.

– I was expecting that, he confessed ruefully.

As we were walking to the car, I asked him if he had any other weirdos like that one tucked away.

– Nah, nothing to write home about. If you like I can take you to meet the owner of the Zoo Sex Club, he's a second dan karate expert, a helluva character, or else a dwarf lady who smokes cigars; you can always find her across from the Hawaii Kai Bar on Broadway. But we won't find out anything else, believe me.

– Then let's go and have a last drink at the Mexico Lindo.

– The last, you swear?

– I swear, Joe, marine's word of honour.

– You don't fool around with a marine's word of honour. At least not when he's still on active service. Laughing, we slapped palms together, like in the good old days. As we were driving along, I told myself I was already getting a better picture of who was coming at me. The little guys in the Last Chance weren't as moderate as Friedman wanted people to believe. Or at any rate their entourage wasn't. And right then I saw the likelihood of the band being party to some pretty vital trafficking – and they had just left for Europe. All this dirty laundry wasn't too happy about a private eye sticking his schozz in, even indirectly, for, until evidence to the contrary, Maria-Liza wasn't mixed up in this for nothing. The only problem was that I'd had my toes stepped on and I had my own scores to settle. Debts shouldn't be left too long. But I knew I'd deal with that sooner or later here in New York. Fact was, either I stayed here and washed my dirty laundry on my own, which wasn't too great for the Tonkin' cleaners, or Daddy Belmont would send me to Europe and things could get ugly. So until the morning it was ceasefire time for me, since my enemies seemed to be pretty well informed about my every move. And during a ceasefire some dig in, and others party.

SEVEN

As parties go, it had been one helluva shindig. At the Mexico Lindo, Joe and I had run into some old mutual friends we hadn't seen since the business of the illegal chicanos. We had celebrated our reunion liquid-style with tequila, and tacos and guacamole on the side, by way of padding. Around 2 a.m. we were still there belting old standards and throwing pounds of salt over our shoulders when Hammer came into the bar. Hammer is one of my old girlfriends, a woman of character with a totally chequered past.

She had started out very young as a high-class hooker and at the same time had come up with an interesting scam that had allowed her to keep her virginity until we met. I'm not claiming that she saved herself for me – I'm the kind who lost my illusions even before I was weaned – but the fact is she still had her cherry on our first date. Through a pimp who had never laid a finger or anything else on her, she had specialised in the tourist-who's-leaving-New-York-tomorrow routine. Once she'd managed to lure the john into her apartment on 59th Street West, she would help herself to his wallet and leave the moron alone with her two dobermans, probably the only two undomesticated dobermans in the whole of the US. At dawn she would call off the monsters while the victim beat a hasty retreat to catch his plane. Respect for either their wives or their reputation, or both, made it extremely rare for any of her clients to go to the police. And if there was a charge laid, there'd be too little evidence; as for who would turn up on the day of the eventual trial, that was even more complicated. She would get back to work the next day, as if nothing had happened, making an annual turnover of around 100,000 dollars.

At the time when we'd met, five or six years earlier, Hammer was flourishing. And the two of us had hit it off right away. She had that invaluable quality in a woman: discretion (as well as having lots of sex appeal). She must have acquired it in her work, and it was all I asked. And so each time we met up again it was a chance encounter that was well worth celebrating. In eight years of whoring, she'd had time to put plenty by, and she lived well, independently, now and then turning a trick just for fun.

So Hammer had landed at the Lindo with no trick in tow, and we'd disappeared shortly after, leaving Joe and the others pretty stewed. I had taken her back to my place, my apartment on 17th East, where I hadn't set foot for nearly a week. It felt a bit unlived in, but it was just what we were looking for. We had a pretty raunchy time, but I'll spare you the details. A man has to know how to maintain discretion regarding certain areas of his private life. At any rate that's always been my point of view.

As a result, for once I had no difficulty recognising the female specimen lying beside me in my kingsize (no filter) bed. Our athletics had worked off the excess tequila, and I didn't have to struggle much to open my

70

eyes. We must have been pretty hot, judging by the path marked out from the door; if you followed it you could pick up a jacket, a suspender belt, the pants that matched the jacket, etc.

I got up and lit up, grabbed a big black towel off the back of the chair and made like a native, then headed for the kitchen, feeling my way gently, granted. I love going home occasionally. It makes me feel like an animal reclaiming its territory. Not that my apartment's particularly luxurious or the decor's artistic, but it's mine and there's nothing to beat that. I slipped a wink at the portrait of Sugar Ray Robinson above the sink as I filled the coffeepot with water. I dumped plenty of ground in the machine and cranked it up. I don't think I could have taken the noise of a grinder so early.

I went back into the living room, drew the curtains to let the light in, and looked at my watch. It was 10.30 already. Sex makes you screw up. I imitated the cry of a plains coyote to wake up Hammer, and she answered with another groan a lot less sensual than the ones last night.

– When it's time to get up, you don't take all day, you just *get up*, I yelled at her by way of a welcome back to the world of consciousness.

– Sam, for Christ's sake just let me sleep, y'jerk!

– No way, baby your stablemates have been out there spreading 'em, and you've done nada yet.

I went back to the kitchen, poured two mugs of steaming coffee and, very courteously, brought one back for her.

– With the compliments of the house.

What was nice about Hammer was that she was as superb in the morning as at night, which is rare, and just the smell of the coffee put her in a good mood. It

71

must have been because of her Brazilian origins. She sat down on the bed, shading her eyes from the white light that flooded the room, and fell greedily on her coffee.

– What a night, Sam, Jeez what a night! There isn't another like you, believe me, she said flatteringly.

This wasn't news to me.

– We'll do it again whenever you like, darling. But for now I've got work waiting for me. So drink up, get dressed and get going, okay? There's a time for everything.

Any other female would have flung her coffee cup at me, or called me names, but Hammer knew me inside out, and it took more than that to offend her.

– Okay, okay, but don't talk so loud, you're giving me a headache.

I plugged in the radio and tuned it to something tolerable. In no time I hit on an old Sinatra number: 'In The Wee Small Hours'. It was very fitting and I've always loved ol' Blue Eyes. When I'd drunk a few mouthfuls of coffee I made a bee-line for the shower and stood under it for fifteen minutes solid. To begin with cold water is kind of unpleasant, then you get used to it and then it starts to feel really nice. I even started singing along with Sinatra as I soaked myself, something I don't do very often: I've a strong dislike for people who sing in the shower. When I went back into the bedroom, rubbing myself dry, Hammer had disappeared, leaving me a note on the bed: 'You know where to find me, don't leave me alone too long.' Alone? Her idea of a desert island would be something like Jamaica or Great Britain.

I allowed myself the luxury of a wet shave, a close one, with a lime foam that retained something of last night's ambience. With my suit and a clean shirt I was a new man.

I rang Belinda.

– Sam! I was worried sick, I've been looking for you everywhere.

– I'm at home, little one.

– Another time I needed your home number. You've always refused to give it to me.

– That's because I'm hardly ever here, Belinda. And when I am I don't want telephone calls, I retorted.

– Okay, Belmont is looking for you everywhere. He's made up his mind you're going to Europe to look for his daughter.

So things *were* going to get ugly. I was ready.

– He's booked you a New York–Paris round trip on TWA flight 0735 at 9 tonight from JFK. The ticket's been paid for, you just have to collect it from the desk an hour before departure. On top of that, you'll find an envelope in your name at the desk containing 2,000 dollars in French francs. Is your passport up to date?

I couldn't remember ever having set foot in France. My father did; he'd landed there a year before I was conceived. As for me, I'd never conceived being able to land there on my own.

– I don't have a visa, but Harry can fix that for me today.

– Another thing, he's booked you a room in the hotel where his daughter is staying. Take the address: Hotel Warwick, rue de Berri.

– Has he spoken to her?

– He rang from New York around midnight. It was dawn in France. She was in her room all right, but a man's voice answered saying she wouldn't speak to him. That's what decided him on sending you there.

Anyway, he'd like to speak to you this afternoon. You can get him at the Plaza at 4.30 sharp.

– Fine, Belinda, let's meet for lunch at 12 at Suerken's; it's at 27 Park Place, near the World Trade Center. I'll have talked to Harry by then and I'll give you my passport. Do you need anything?

– No thanks, Sam, see you at 12. And be careful.

– Don't worry, it's second nature. See you later.

I got in touch with Harry right after and gave him the lowdown. I nearly fell over backwards when he announced that he'd just decided that very minute to fly out with me. He explained that for the last couple of months he'd kept putting off a decision about some vacation time he had owing. I'd acted as a catalyst, he tried to explain, with what I thought was a hint of irony. Another thing, he argued, he knew Paris very well and spoke French almost fluently. What it came down to was him and the visa, or nothing at all. With great reluctance I yielded to his argument, and grumbled an 'okay' so unconvincing it would have nixed admission to the Actors Studio for a whole generation. He would wait for Belinda to bring him the passport. I hung up gloomily.

I left my place with two dirty shirts under my arm and made a detour to the Tonkin'. The news of my departure, albeit temporary, nearly killed them, and it was in voices racked with sobs that they wished me 'a happy and estimable journey'.

I jumped into a taxi – this guy only played funk and drove with his knees to leave his hands free for clapping – and got to my restaurant meeting five minutes ahead of time. I took a table next to a huge mural depicting marine life and ordered mucho coffee to whet my appetite.

I was about to light a coffin nail when Belinda, the

patron saint of punctuality, made her entrance. She looked very nervous, as if she was the one leaving that night.

– Sam, have you thought about filing a complaint about what happened at the office, she asked as she sat down.

– Complaints are for me to collect, I won't have any fun making them too, I said soothingly.

– You're not being serious, Sam, I'm thinking of the insurance.

From that point of view it certainly made more sense.

– Be a good girl and take care of it while I'm away.

She agreed resignedly. When I'd checked with her I ordered some clams, prawns, crab salad and brew. I handed her my passport and scribbled an address on a match cover.

– Take this to Harry Marotta; this is his address. You'll need to get it back by late afternoon. Harry is leaving with me, but I prefer to have it in my own hands. Would you mind meeting me around 8 at Kennedy?

– Not at all Sam!

As we ate lunch we exchanged views on the case and on Paris. She had always dreamt of going to Paris. Within half an hour we'd disposed of all the food, and she took to studying the paper place mats. They showed aeroplanes of all different kinds, with explanations of how they manage to fly, which is something I'll never understand.

– What a coincidence, she said, amazed.

– You can take it that way, I admitted, but I don't believe in coincidences or in chance.

I cut short a promising line of conversation and got the bill, then we parted on the sidewalk. I went back home to get a few things ready and check up on a few things, like my bank balance, and more importantly, my Magnum. They were both a bit sticky, but the latter only needed a few drops of oil. For safety's sake I took the whole thing apart, oiled all the pieces, checked the barrel and the safety, and loaded it with six Quick Defense candies, which would make its tummy feel less empty. I set aside some ammo for the trip. These are bullets it's not very easy to get hold of. And, like the Boy Scouts say, Be Prepared. I'd wait until check-in at the airport before I stowed my weapon in my travel bag. I packed a few shirts, another suit and some underwear.

Around 3 I made a call to Joe's office. His secretary told me he'd just woken up and that apparently he'd slept under his desk. Ruth wouldn't be the one turning up at the airport with a kidnap plan to stop me from leaving. Joe's voice was barely audible.

– What a bender, gee what a bender, old buddy! Do you know what? I should give up on tequila!

– Try vodka, old soak, I advised.

– Ruth is mad as hell, she's talking about going back to her mother. My goodness! You should have heard her, he guffawed.

He seemed out of synch.

– Joe, the devil is flying out to Paris tonight, you can go on the wagon.

– No kidding, Sam Murchison in the land of the froggies. Oh, I'd love to see that.

– Come along, if you like the idea, I suggested.

– No thanks, not on your life! I'm holding on to what's left of my liver. Hey, you don't speak a word of their filthy language, how are you going to get by?

– I've a real gift for languages, I improvised. Anyway, Harry has decided to come with me and he speaks the lingo.

76

– He's decided he wants to die in Europe?

– No, to take a vacation, which amounts to much the same thing.

– Well, that's your goose cooked. Hold on, he added, there's a guy I know over there. Cardier. Pierre Cardier, do you remember he was a correspondent with AFP in New York at the end of the war.

Sure, Cardier! A tall, skinny guy, kinda nice, we'd hung out with him for a few months. Joe had stayed in touch with him, and he'd even seen him two or three times on some of his shady trips to Europe.

– Hang on, I've got his number somewhere.

He put the phone down and I heard him swear as he knocked over a chair. It took him three minutes plus to find his little book.

– Right, take this down, he said, and gave me a Paris number.

– Pierre is totally bilingual and he'll be able to give you a hand. Particularly since he's still a journalist and your story might interest him. Imagine the headlines: 'American Private Eye in Paris'!

– I'm not exactly going there to give a press conference, but I promise I'll call him.

– Sam?

– Yes.

– Watch your step, and don't forget I'm here, okay?

I thanked him not once but three times – he wouldn't let me hang up – and finished packing. It was a little after 3, and I didn't have much to do until 4.30. I switched on the TV and channel-hopped until I came across the end of a match between the Dodgers and the Black Arrows. The Dodgers were giving the Black Arrows a helluva beating. Naturally. There was a rock programme on after the commercials, and I was just about to switch channels when I heard the name of the Last Chance Band trailed. I turned up the volume right away, grabbed a beer from the fridge without taking my eyes off the screen and settled into the only armchair in the room.

I had to sit through a whole string of bands before getting to the one that interested me. There was something for everybody. Hard, soft, pastel-coloured, black and white, grey, comedians and sermonisers, sad guys and decidedly bad guys, and guys who were maybe glad to be gay. They all segued on smoothly, with an MC for whom each group was the greatest, which amounted to saying they were all the same – entirely depending on where you were standing. Finally, I was allowed the Last Chance.

They made their appearance in a film where you saw them exploding mirrors, knocking over glasses of champagne in slow motion and watching eagles fly. It was the backdrop to the song; this told in detail the tale of a guy whose girlfriend has run away with his best friend and he's wondering whether in the end life isn't just like having a bath in a cesspool. Deeply symbolic. They all had highly studied facial expressions and very elaborate haircuts. Joe de Brown was nearly always shot in close-up, which gave me plenty of time to check him out. He was gesticulating all over the place to get his stuff across, and the least you could say is that he had looks. He was fixed up with a profile that wasn't too unlike the one the eagle had in the film, the kind that makes mothers lock up their daughters when he's in the vicinity. The idol, the ladykiller. Health-wise, I'd have bet 1,000 dollars that he didn't do the pentathlon every day. He was more of the hollow-eyed, self-consuming type. But people eat what there is to hand and appropriately, he kept on covering up his face behind his mitts. He must have had an itch. At a rough guess he was about six feet without heels, and an eighth of this in width. In fact it was hard to say whether he was full-face or profile. But what he had most of all was a kind of strange magnetism which must have made women melt. As for the music, I have to admit I was pleasantly surprised. It wasn't too different from some of the black soul music I'd liked listening to in the sixties. The image had changed a lot, no doubt about that. The music much less so. But after all, the world goes round and I don't see why people shouldn't do the same.

When the music was over, I got an interview which focussed mainly on their trip to Europe. Why were they more popular over there? 'Undoubtedly because they have more taste in Europe,' was de Brown's straightforward answer. I kind of liked him for it. Not for what he'd said, but for the way he'd put it. I love a touch of provocation. The interviewer liked it much less, because he thanked him somewhat coldly before going on to the next item. I switched off. The time had come to call Belmont.

– Murchison, I was expecting you. Has your secretary told you what I decided?

– Absolutely, Mr Belmont.

– And it's okay with you?

– Of course, I confirmed. I can't stand leaving a case unsolved.

– Fine, your ticket's ready, along with the 2,000 dollars. And I've made you an open booking with Hertz in case you need a car. You can hire one anywhere any time.

– My secretary told me you'd talked to Maria-Liza?

– That's right. She was indeed registered at the hotel with this de Brown, and I woke them up. It must have been 3 a.m. I heard her voice, then the receiver was clearly pulled out of her hand. A man's voice told me quite brutally that she had nothing to say to me and to leave them alone. I can't make this out, and my wife is terribly worried.

– I understand, Mr Belmont. Do you know how long they're staying in Paris?

– Three or four days, I'm not sure. In any case they'll still be there when you arrive.

– Fine, I'll call you tomorrow evening.

– I'm going back to Miami tonight, call me there.

– Okay, and don't worry too much, I lied.

– Good luck, Murchison, and do what's best.

– As ever, I tried wisecracking, but the tone of the conversation wasn't jocular.

I had a bit less than three hours left before leaving for the airport. I decided to take a much needed catnap. Joe still hadn't got home and, for him, the real party hadn't started yet. As for mine, I won't even mention it.

EIGHT

For the trip to the airport I was blessed with John Templeman, ex-director of a company that made washing-machine parts turned cab driver. He'd tried everything, he told me, from sexy lingerie to double glazing, by way of gaskets and modern art lithographs. But he'd never had a head for business and, he said, 'competition's cruel here.' Happily, he hadn't given up the ghost, and he recited the list of his projects for me. He had notions for importing bananas, manufacturing custom-made hub-caps, or else a new revolutionary toothbrush that cleaned the teeth and the gums simultaneously. 'The taxi's a stopgap,' he wound up with a perfect sense of timing, just as we arrived at JFK. As I gave him his tip it felt as if I was contributing to the relaunch of small industry. At least it would buy him a drink while he waited for something better to come along.

Belinda was waiting for me as arranged at the TWA desk. She'd got my passport back minus Harry, who was still nowhere to be seen. But I wasn't going to have him paged. I picked up the envelope with the ticket and the dough in it. Belmont wasn't doing things by halves. I had a seat in Ambassador class.

Before checking in, I slid my Magnum discreetly to the bottom of my bag, and passed them both on to a stunning stewardess. I promised Belinda I'd keep her informed daily, on condition she didn't stir from home.

– I'll miss you, Sam, she confessed.

It was the first time a case had taken me so far away.

– You miss a single being, and the whole world is empty, I told her sagely. But I don't think it'll take me very long. You haven't mislaid the address of my hotel in Paris?

– Of course not!

– Don't give it to anybody but Joe Mangelson. Got me?

– Okay Sam.

She looked upset. To her delight I planted a chaste kiss on her upper lip. She started blushing.

– Take care, won't you?

This was getting to be a habit. She went with me as far as the customs barrier and I left her with an affectionate little wave. I stocked up on newspapers for the plane. I treated myself to the *Post*, the *New York Times*, the new *Playboy* and the latest *Handgun Bible*. After all the departure formalities I settled comfortably into my seat to wait for take-off. The flight captain's voice boomed out through the cabin and I nearly spilt my first Scotch when he told us his name. It was James Blackwell, another veteran of the Vietnam vacation. No doubt about it, I was running into them everywhere. In those days he was the world champion helicopter pilot, and he'd got us out of some pretty tight spots often enough. He was a helicopter ace: freestyle or fancy, there was nothing he didn't do, until the day he had to make a crash landing in the middle of the jungle. That had left him in bad shape and he'd been repatriated to neutral territory, an Australian base where he'd stayed on. Since then we'd only met once six years before, for a reunion feed. I sincerely hoped he'd fly his 747s more smoothly than his choppers, but it wouldn't take long before I found out. I took some paper and wrote him a note and asked the stewardess if she'd be good enough to take it to him.

Blackwell had always been on the exuberant side, and I was only slightly surprised to hear a roar through the loudspeakers interrupting the syrupy muzak.

– Murchison! Sam Murchison! You old stinker, what's keeping you, come and have a snifter up front, ha! ha! ha! . . .

Laughing too, I got up and headed towards the cockpit under the inquisitive eye of the other passengers. (Very few people know that pilots hit the bottle in a big way.)

He was in the middle of checking a vast array of monitors when I landed in his rathole. He got up at once and bent his six-foot-six frame to give me a bear hug that buckled my shoulderblades. He hadn't really aged. Altitude must keep people young.

– So I'm flying you on a mission like in the old days, he kidded.

– If you like, but this time nothing is going to make me jump out before we land, I said, going along with the joke.

– Ha, ha, ha, you never know, Sam, you never know, with these crappy machines and all their electronic doodads, he said, as if he wanted to reassure me. Listen, I gotta get busy raising this old hulk. Go back to your seat, and as soon as we're horizontal we'll celebrate, okay?

83

This didn't seem to go down well with the radio operator, who looked like one of those sensitive types who go through life in a withdrawn silence, but we weren't asking for his opinion. So I went back to my seat for take-off. The plane was pretty full and if Blackwell's promises were to be believed it wouldn't be long before I was myself. But that's still the best way anybody ever came up with of spending a few hours getting high, in both senses. Up or down, same difference. As soon as I could get out of my seat and move around, I went to look for Harry. But I scoured every single row in vain; he wasn't to be found. He must have missed the flight.

Jimmy kept his promise, and we spent the best part of the seven-hour flight reminiscing. And believe me, we weren't harking back to our first communion or the style of clothes we wore in the late sixties. No! More like memories of hell, which, despite everything, became almost beautiful. That's to say a kind of savage beauty, there's no disguising it. At any rate, I missed a real turkey of a movie – the plot was about a fisherman whose wife leaves him while he's at sea and who ends up running a bar for lumberjacks in Wisconsin so as to forget women and their cruelty. But apparently he doesn't get along with the local big wheels so he starts hitting the bottle. This goes on until another chick gives him a yen for the high seas again and saves him from a shipwreck. The film hadn't been a great success when it came out in the movie theatres – to tell the truth, it was more like the audiences who were coming out of the movie theatres – and that's probably why they showed it as inflight entertainment, in front of a captive, though hardly captivated audience.

Before landing Blackwell gave me the number of the

hotel where he spent his stopovers in Paris and where I could reach him two or three times in a week. He made me promise we'd spend an evening painting the town red. 'If you can't do that in this damned city, I ask myself where can you do it, ha, ha!' I agreed, having no objection. We landed just like in the good old days. 'Give these yellow livers a good shake, that'll wake them up,' Jimmy had told me by way of warning.

I left the airport without a hitch, and they didn't even ask me to open my bag at customs. I was flabbergasted by this casual attitude but I didn't go so far as to take offence. I'd scribbled the address of the hotel on a piece of paper and I handed this to the first cabbie who was free. I settled down comfortably enough inside his little buggy and gave myself over to taking in the scenery. I had plenty of time to check it all out since he took me on a full-length guided tour before I reached my destination. All the freshness and enthusiasm of delighted discovery was mine as I gazed at each and every landmark in the city. It was amazing that they were all on the way. Finally he stopped in front of the Warwick and made me pay a fare a family of Puerto Ricans could have lived on for at least five years.

With my watch changed to French time it was 10 a.m. when I asked reception for my room key. There was a message from Harry waiting for me, short and sweet: 'I'll be there later today.'

Once again Belmont had done things in style and booked me a suite of rooms with a kingsize bed. I took a long shower so as to collect my thoughts, then had some coffee sent up. It was real coffee, not the diluted New York kind, and I realised I'd have to cut down unless I wanted to find out what a heart attack was like. Half an hour later I was on the offensive, asking reception to put me through to de Brown's room. The switchboard told me it was impossible. They'd asked not to be disturbed before noon. I asked for the room number. She refused once again, politely. This was a fine start! Maintaining my cool, I kept on quizzing the stickler of a telephonist. If I couldn't talk directly to the artistes, there must be somebody in the entourage who'd be able to tell me what I wanted to know. For the first time I got a positive answer.

– Oh yes, there's the tour manager, Mr Turner, but he won't be very pleased to be woken up.

– If that's the only thing he has to worry about in this world of ours, then he's a happy man. Put me through to him right away, I ordered.

My ears started burning when I was treated to a series of asides on how these Yanks were making her life impossible, then I was transferred and there was a loud ringing in my left ear, the side I was holding the receiver on. On the sixth ring somebody answered with a litany of insults too crude to be reproduced here, e.g. 'Dirty little son-of-a-bitch motherfucker.'

– Delighted, I answered, Sam Murchison, I'd like to speak to Mr Turner.

– Murchison? Who's that? the voice roared.

– I've just got in from New York, and I've been engaged by Mr Belmont to take his daughter home, are you with me?

He wasn't. I tried again.

– New York. Belmont. Maria-Liza. Daddy and Mummy are looking for her. Me take her home.

– Listen, buddy, the voice answered, I don't like jokers disturbing my beauty rest. There's no daughter here and Turner isn't here either, so get lost.

The phone was hung up. I called the switchboard

to get them to put me through again, and I gave Turner's name again.

– It wasn't Mr Turner? Then I don't know where he is. Try again later.

It was tough, and if it meant being given the run-around just to get hold of the guy who'd seen the guy who'd seen the guy who'd seen the daughter, I'd be better off learning some new rules. I decided to wait until noon. And rather than waste time, I ordered myself ham and eggs, four of them, a half chicken in aspic, and a few beers. While I was waiting for the grub I had a wander round my suite and took a look out of the window. Paris looked pocket-sized cute, with its buildings made for dwarfs, its streets as wide as my office and its cars three and a half times the size of Dinky toys. Lovely town. I wondered if they had the same scale models for people somewhere. I made a call to Cardier, who wasn't asleep, hadn't changed his room and was even at his desk. He made me repeat my name three times. Finally it came to him.

– No, I don't believe it, Sam. Come on, where are you calling from?

– From Paris, France.

– How come? You're in Paris! he reiterated with an accent you could cut with a knife. But how did you manage to find me?

I explained.

– Joe, of course, well I never! Where are you staying? At the Warwick? Great! You're here on business? Wonderful!

I couldn't get a word in.

– Listen, I'm up to my ears in it, I've got a deadline for 2 o'clock. But I'll call you this afternoon. Have fun, Sam Murchison.

He seemed just as excitable and effusive as a decade

ago, in the days when he'd listened open-mouthed to our war stories, expressing his amazement with a running commentary of exclamations.

There was a knock at my door. It was the chicken and the eggs, followed by the floor waiter. I checked the chicken to make sure it was really the waiter who'd knocked, but it didn't move. Nor did the waiter, but he was waiting for his tip. I slipped him a frogskin, then he thanked me and took himself off.

I threw myself at my breakfast like a Queens street gang mugging a junior executive. They'd done my eggs sunny side up, which any Navajo indian would have taken as a good sign. I reduced the chicken to a heap of bones and downed one of the beers in one. Almost at once I felt the onset of fatigue and I crashed on the bed to get a little rest. It was the telephone that woke me. I was somewhat less than happy to see it was already 4 p.m. Cardier was on the line.

– Jetlag, Sam, he said sagely, jetlag.

But this didn't calm me down. He asked me quickly about the precise purpose of my visit to Paris. I explained even faster. He seemed taken aback.

– Good heavens! A private eye! It takes you Yanks to come up with these things!

– So long as there are mugs making trouble for other mugs there'll always be private dicks needed to clean up after them, I told him. Which means it'll be a while before I find myself out of work.

That made him laugh. He said he'd drop by to say hello tomorrow, which happened to be his day off. I woke up properly under a Niagara-force shower, shaved, splashed on some eau de cologne, cleaned my pearly white teeth and put on a fresh outfit, once more courtesy of Tonkin'.

With the minimum of fuss I landed at reception,

where I picked up my winding trail again from scratch. This time around I was out of luck. There was nobody from the band in the hotel, neither technician nor musicians. They'd all gone off to set things up for the gig. They were playing that evening at 8 in a joint called the Casino de Paris. I knew that casinos were for gambling, I didn't know they were for music. It had to be one of the local customs. I asked for the address and was just dashing out when I ran straight into Harry, preceded by a porter and several suitcases.

– So, reprobate, you've already forgotten me? You thought I was maybe going to leave you all on your own in gay Paree?

I'd completely forgotten about Harry. But if I'd cherished the slightest hope of not seeing him – something that hadn't even crossed my mind – I might as well forget it. He took advantage of my surprise to give me a few hefty claps on the back. Any more of this, and I'd be ready to be repatriated by the Red Cross. But Harry, as usual, showed himself yet again to be more shrewd than affectionate.

– Well, I see you're not altogether on your own, he observed, feeling the butt of my Magnum which was tucked into the waistband of my pants.

– You well know that I never leave him, Harry, he's completely neurotic.

– You may laugh, Sam, but remember that your licence to carry a weapon is worth as much as a subway token here. You're an ordinary citizen just like everybody else in this city.

Harry couldn't resist doling out advice all the time. And even though he was well aware of its effect on me, he couldn't help himself. But on that particular day I was in no mood for advice, even from a buddy.

– Just leave the two of us to it, Harry, and you'd

better hurry up and register, I think the hotel's booked up.

– Don't worry on my account, I've had my reservation confirmed, he said, heading for reception. And if you wait five minutes, I'll be with you, he added.

– Hey! You surely don't think you're going to be my chaperone, Harry, I'm here on a case, not a guided tour.

– Calm down Sam, you don't speak a word of this damned language and you can't imagine what's in store for a naive foreigner like you round here. I'm only telling you as a friend, and you know me: I can be discreet when the need arises, can't I?

I did know him, and his discretion was proverbial. At any rate, I'd never had to complain about it. And there was nothing scary lurking round the corner. I had to go to a concert and talk to a teenager who was giving Mummy and Daddy a lot of heartache and, eventually, take her by the hand and bring her home. Nothing special. I have to admit that at that moment, seen from Paris, the snags I'd run up against in New York were becoming almost unreal, intangible. Everything seemed relatively simple. Anyway, Harry had smoothed things out for my visa, I couldn't deny him something in return.

– Okay, Harry, it's fine for today, but don't cramp my style when I really get going.

He agreed with a smile I obviously shouldn't have trusted. But whether it was the effect of the jetlag, or the inflight bender, combined with a touch of nervous exhaustion, I just wasn't up to arguing, and I *was* fond of him.

I decided I'd wait for him on one of the deep lobby sofas while he left his luggage. During this brief lull I worked out that I could in fact easily wind up the case that very evening, one way or another. Get little Liza to a phone and make her explain herself to her folks, and steer her back to the US tomorrow, after a bit of persuasion. I was even just about convinced I was going to spoil Harry's vacation by leaving him all on his own. But I've never been much good at fortune-telling.

NINE

It was a little after 7.30 when the cab dropped us at the Casino de Paris. The street was jammed with two lines of cars and part of the crowd was pushing up against the railings. This resulted in an infernal racket, a mixture of car horns and protests Harry said were because of a delay in opening the doors. Getting to the entrance was out of the question, especially since there was a relentless downpour drenching everything in sight. I dragged him into the first bar we came to, on the other side of the road. I'd never set foot in a French bar before, and I have to say I was a bit surprised. A dim light was shed on a tiny tiled room crowded with people all talking as if to drown out the noise of two pinball machines that were going haywire. I couldn't make out a word of this loud, mangled language, but I soon got the impression that they were all ordering drinks, going by the rate at which glasses of beer were landing on the counter. It was mostly young kids who'd had the same idea as us, to get wet inside rather than outside. Leather seemed to be very much in vogue, and Harry and I in our straight suits looked like a couple of fashionplates from the distant past. I was going to attempt communication with the owner of the joint when Harry told me people were starting to go into the hall. We rushed outside to join the tide of fans and five minutes later found ourselves face to face with two gorillas whose job consisted of tearing up tickets. We didn't have any. Harry asked if we could buy them at the box office, but the curt answer was that the concert was sold out. He embarked on a spiel that looked to me like an attempt at negotiation, but the two apes weren't interested. The crowd behind us was beginning to get fractious. I could feel we were about to run out of steam when Harry hit on the magic words that let us inside the lobby. He'd claimed we were on some list. We were Americans and this seemed plausible to the two bruisers, but the box office confirmed that all the tickets were sold, and we had repeat our act again with two other elephants who were a lot less chatty than the first two. All the kids were going past us while we two were stuck there at the top of some steps that led into the Casino. After a minute of this I'd had enough.

– Tell those two deadheads that either they let us in or we let them have it, I muttered. I get edgy.

One of the two King Kongs must have had a spell as a language student in the free world for he adopted a nasty tone of voice and told me to go and fuck myself, preferably with my mother. He accompanied this threat with a tug on the lapel of my jacket, a gesture I interpreted as totally unwarranted aggression. Truth be told, no sooner had he touched me than I made him suddenly aware of his manhood, and how hard it would be for him to make use of it for the next few days. While he was bent double screaming I took the opportunity to help him up, and pitched his head back against one of the glass panes of the door, nearly

93

shattering it. Not quite, but the glass splintered all the same. By all appearances this wasn't the kind of sporting encounter appreciated by his cronies, because in two seconds flat Harry and I found ourselves surrounded by six of them. *They* were threatening. In a flash Harry pulled out his badge. It must have been a conditioned reflex, since less than an hour ago he'd been telling me that I, and he by the same token, was a citizen like any other in this burg. In any case, his bit of metal had as much effect on them as a Swiss German customs strike. They were ready to lunge, and we were ready to catch them. In any case it was going to get ugly. Suddenly a voice was raised above the impending fracas, and the would-be participants in the slaughter stopped dead in their tracks. A guy with glasses appeared, looking worried, and came right up to us asking for an explanation. He was treated first to the version of one of the bouncers who pointed emphatically to his colleague, then to me, then back to his colleague. The guy would have had a great career as a mime artist and I couldn't stop myself from applauding when the performance was over. I might add he did well to speak up for his pal, since the other guy was still rolling around on the floor alternately clutching at his groin and his head. Then Harry explained, running through more or less the same set of gestures indicating victim and perpetrator. I used the pause to light a cigarette. The character he was telling all this to – he was the concert promoter, Harry told me later – looked as if he wanted to cool the whole thing. He sent the big apes back to their posts, but that didn't stop them from shooting us looks more poisonous than a nest of rattlesnakes, and I even got the impression he was apologising to us for the incident. This was confirmed when I saw him handing Harry

94

two passes for the gig and showing us inside hospita-
bly. As we went in I asked Harry to share the secret
words he had whispered in the promoter's ear. He
told me he'd improvised a story about Interpol, a drug
network, a suspect in the crowd, etc., giving the guy
assurances that neither his concert nor his organisa-
tion were involved. But that they could be if they kept
on handing out that kind of welcome. I wanted to take
my hat off to him, and only then noticed that I'd left it
at the hotel. It clearly wasn't a day for keeping my
head. Which wasn't as serious as it might have been,
since I didn't have a hat either.

I could see only one likely explanation for the name
Casino: some particularly lucky patron had recently
broken the bank, for the place was so dilapidated it
was almost pathetic. Or else this was an old warehouse for broken-down plumbing fittings re-named
by a manager with a sense of humour. Anyway, the
place was packed solid, from the front row to the
balcony, and a stifling, clammy heat pervaded it. A
low buzz of sound spread through the Casino as the
audience kept on coming in, filling every available
inch of space. It was getting to be like the movie
Exodus when the lights went down, opening the
floodgates to a clamour of satisfaction that was thoroughly genuine. The Last Chance came on stage. The
band was proving to be very popular on this side of
the Atlantic; they'd hardly struck the first chord when
the audience's shouts drowned out everything, and
this went on throughout the first half of their first
number. The volume was breaking all records, which
seemed to keep everybody happy. The musicians
were clearly basking in the glory and were hoisting
their arms in time with the music to show their delight
at being back in the city, as de Brown closed in on his

microphone looking intense yet pooped. As if to show that he wasn't, he yelled a 'Hi there, Paris' at the end of the first song. 'It's great to be back. We're going to give you a hell of a concert, and you won't forget it for a while, oh no!!!' His little introduction unleashed a new wave of rapture which drew in return a drumbeat that was reminiscent of a rhinoceros charge across a field.

Buffeted as we were by this human tide – high tide – this was when Harry and me started feeling like we were gasping for breath. We could scarcely make an inch by now and our only chance of survival was to allow ourselves to be carried every which way like a pedal craft on a swelling sea. As one we decided to head for the healthier air of the shore, and started swimming for the lobby, propelling ourselves with our elbows.

If there were a lot of people in the hall there were nearly as many in the bar, which we finally reached, getting there feeling as good as the mug in the Guinness Book of Records who's just broken all records for eating hardboiled eggs. Harry ordered two beers, across the shoulders of a group of youths who were engaged in a somewhat desultory conversation. I couldn't make out what all those people were doing there. I asked Harry what he thought. After eavesdropping for a couple of minutes he told me peremptorily:

– They're journalists apparently. They're discussing the merits of the Last Chance. It's the same everywhere, the freeloaders meet up in the bar.

– Is that the title of a new movie? I surmised.

I tried to understand how they could be discussing the band out here while they were playing in there, but I soon gave up. It was no skin off my nose.

– Listen, I said, we'll wait for the end of the show

then we'll slip backstage. Anyhow, it's physically impossible to clear a space through the hall unless we set fire to it.

And we could follow the concert just as well from there as from inside. The music filtered through to us almost intact, at any rate decidedly more tolerably than at the centre of the furnace.

The Last Chance was running through what must have been its entire repertoire, with the same kind of ovations greeting the end of each number. Down in the bar, they were prattling away non-stop. From what I could see, the drinks were on the house for all these self-important nobodies, and they were knocking back the free booze with a seriousness and an application that would have come close to perfection if it had been in the nature of work. But where there's life there's parasites, which could be taken as a hopeful sign in this pitiless world.

The concert went on and on. The kids were getting their money's worth. Not one or two, but three curtain calls wound up what would be agreed as from tomorrow as a 'total triumph', and the doors were finally opened again to disgorge the paying public in compact clusters. The scribblers in the bar stayed there a bit longer to let themselves be admired by those who devotedly followed their bylines, and ten minutes or so later it seemed less like hara-kiri to try and make our way towards the front of the hall. If you could still call it a hall. If the proprietors were reckoning on doing more shows there, they'd do better to envisage things like the annual firework-makers ball. It wasn't in good shape before, it wasn't in any shape at all now. Thousands of greasy papers, not so greasy papers, non-greasy papers, cigarette butts and beer bottles littered the floor and what were once the seats. On stage a group of technicians had already started dismantling things, and there was a bleak party's over atmosphere. But whole books have already been written about this kind of stuff.

Being no strangers to swamps, in no time we found our way into the wings, which once again were guarded by a heavy from the goon squad. This time there wasn't the slightest snag, thanks to the promoter's pass. The guardian of the sacred place wasn't exactly itching for trouble, even though I discerned a hint of mistrust in the look he gave us, if look's the right word. Nor was backstage anything like Death Valley. There was a crowd consisting of some incredibly badly dressed women, some of our neighbours from the bar who were still holding forth imperturbably, as well as roadies and other more unlikely characters equally in attendance. In fact the joint was jumping. I tried looking for Maria-Liza's pretty puss in the crowd but I saw nothing there that looked remotely like her. Harry asked me what the singer's name was again, then he intercepted one of the Americans in charge of the equipment. He told us we should find Turner, who would be somewhere by the dressing rooms. Good old Turner . . . . He was just the way I'd pictured him.

Middling build, thick-set, moustached and nervy; I saw right away that we weren't destined to become the best of friends.

– So you're the famous Murchinson, he remarked, making his first mistake.

– CHISON, not Murchinson. I'm flattered that my notoriety has reached you, it's always encouraging.

I got the impression he'd have been happier with just my notoriety. My physical presence seemed to disconcert him altogether.

98

– Friedman warned me you might show up, he admitted, but I think you've made your trip for nothing. Maria-Liza is a big girl and you can't make her leave Joe. In any case, you're not going to meet her, and she has no wish to see you.

– If she's as big as all that, she can tell me herself, I retorted with conviction.

He wasn't convinced.

– Listen, Murchison, you can do your job your way when you're on home ground. You can amuse yourself being a pain in the ass all over Manhattan, but here, maybe you haven't realised, we're in Europe. And nobody here gives a damn about you. Get it?

My knuckles were beginning to itch again. Harry intervened.

– Let me introduce myself: Harry Marotta, 10th Precinct. I'm travelling with Murchison as a friend, and you're right: neither of us have any authority here at all. All you're being asked is to tell us where Maria-Liza is. Sam just wants to talk to her. I think that reasonable, don't you?

Turner's tone altered slightly.

– Mr Marotta, I've had orders from my boss in New York. It's simple, I have to do whatever's necessary to stop Murchison from going near de Brown and Maria-Liza. You see, apart from any legalities, we're at the start of a very important tour, and . . . .

– Yeah, we know, fragile equilibrium . . . . I interrupted. Spare us the sermon, Turner, I've already had it from your boss. I want to talk to Maria-Liza, whether you like it or not. To be honest with you, you mean as much to me as the Statue of Liberty does in the Kremlin. (I was pleased with this image; I'd come up with it on the spur of the moment.) So either you tell me where she is and pronto or I'm going to get annoyed. You've only seen my good side, Turner.

But he was the kind of guy who only gets impressed when he's missing teeth. And for my part, in spite of the crazy urge I had, I couldn't spend the whole evening beating up on everyone who came along. Particularly since Turner could still be useful. However, he had enough intelligence left to see what was coming, and he got out of it the best way he could.

– Okay, I'm certainly not going to stick my neck out for that slut. Wait back here, and I'll come for you when things have quietened down. For the moment the musicians are still in their dressing rooms and nobody can go in there. Will that do?

It would do, although I felt this sudden about-turn didn't bode well. We took ourselves into the corner, hangdog in the midst of the general good humour. We were a couple of killjoys in the middle of a feverishly excited little scene where everyone was relishing and drawing attention to the privilege of being right at the heart of the action. As far as I was concerned, the action was beginning to be sadly lacking. It's a job where you have to know how to wait. I've never known.

TEN

At least fifteen minutes went by before Turner came back. He seemed preoccupied, as if he had some bad news to tell us. The place had cleared a bit and there were only a dozen or so groupies twittering to themselves.

– I'm terribly sorry, but de Brown and Maria-Liza have disappeared. They went off in their limousine as soon as the curtain came down. I was sure they were still in the dressing room with the others.

Harry shot me a look of dismay. Turner had taken us for a ride. Without taking my eyes off Harry, I reached out towards the tour manager's neck and brought his florid face within an inch of mine. Then I looked him straight in the eyes, with a stare like an ice-cold blade, and lifted him off the floor, bringing him up to normal height.

– Listen jerk, I muttered, eyeball to eyeball, so far I've managed to restrain myself and you can consider yourself lucky. You're now going to tell me double quick where they are and why you think you can treat me like shit.

He was all choked up and the pressure of my fist stopped him from speaking clearly.

– I . . . sw . . . swear . . . .

I let him breathe a little, but without giving him permission to hit floor level yet.

– Don't get . . . so . . . het up, he panted. I'm not lying . . . I was sure they were all here . . . . Believe me, I swear to you . . . .

I dropped him and shoved him against the wall that was a yard or so behind him. He rolled his big scared eyes, as if he'd had a narrow escape from death, which was true. I went on:

– And of course you don't have the slightest idea where they've gone?

– Usually we'd meet up with them at the dinner the recording company lays on. But I can't swear to that.

He was on the point of never swearing to anything again.

– Ever since he met the kid Joe's become totally unpredictable.

– We'll predict for him. Give me the address of the restaurant.

He reacted just as if I'd asked him to go and get me a chilli in San Antonio and bring it back hot.

– Oh no, Murchison, that's going too far. There are some things you have to stay out of. They're having dinner with the managing director of their European company and some people from the press. You can't just barge in on that.

Harry was laughing to himself in his corner.

– Shouldn't ever say a thing like that to Sam. He can never stop himself from doing the opposite of what people tell him.

– No, no. Put yourself in my place. I'd be risking my job if I pulled anything like that, he said, trying to argue.

102

– That's okay, we're in a Casino, I said by way of consolation. Go for the bank, Turner, or I'll make you lick that wall clean.

I went a step or two closer. That was enough to convince him. Grudgingly.

– Christ, what a shitty job. I spend my whole life covering up for everybody else.

– Every job has its place. The address, Turner, make it snappy.

– Okay, okay, he said, taking a sheet of paper out of his pocket and consulting it. I tore it out of his hands and dragged Harry over at the same time.

– I hope for your sake we find them soon, I shot back at Turner, otherwise I'll help you find a new career as blotting paper. Sometimes you need to move on.

We crossed the hall in the opposite direction, taking our leave of what was left of the bouncer fraternity. There were still a lot of people outside in front of the stage door. Two limousines were waiting at the kerb, their engines running. The fans had quietened down. But not the rain. I glanced inside the two cars, whose only occupants were the drivers. I tapped on the window of the front car to ask if a third limousine had left the Casino fifteen minutes earlier. He happened to speak English and told me one had. I thanked him and went to find Harry, who'd taken shelter in a doorway at a distance from the fans. I unfolded Turner's sheet of paper and handed it to him.

– Any idea where it is, this eatery?

He looked at the address and thought for a moment or two, then snapped his fingers.

– No problem, it's near the Bastille, one of the most famous brasseries in Paris.

I silently admired his memory and sense of direc-

103

tion. After all, he'd only twice set foot in this city, where nothing's in a straight line. The architects round here must have been in a hell of a mess when they drew up the plans.

We had to wait a good while before getting hold of a taxi. No sooner had I opened the door than a huge German Shepherd reared up on the front seat so as we could admire the condition of his fangs.

– Don't worry, the driver told us, he does that with everybody, he won't bite. Down, Grem!

His pooch must have been rolling in an overflowing gutter, such was the smell of wet dog. And the two of us were jammed in the back seat with our legs tucked sideways, unable to move except for our hands. It wasn't a car, it was a sardine can.

– From back here you'd hardly know he was really eating up the gas, I said to Harry, indicating the driver.

– It's one of the charms of Europe, Sam. Here things still have a human scale.

– The only problem is that not all humans are built on the same scale, I quipped.

Still, there was the advantage of avoiding unending conversations with chatty drivers.

– Are you strangers? Grem's owner tried out his English.

I took care of the answer. In French.

– Nan! Nous sent améwouicains. Mais vous pas pawler un mot sinon danger, OK?

The literal meaning escaped him, but he got the message and shut up for the rest of the ride. Harry let out a little whistle of admiration. I was making good progress.

The brasserie looked AOK. In the first place you could walk through it without bumping into the tables and, best of all, there was room to breathe. Huge

104

mirrors on the walls expanded the sense of space, while plants, statues and décor gave it a little turn of the century touch. There were quite a lot of people, but we had no trouble spotting the Last Chance table. At least half the journalists were there along with a bunch of three-piece suits, and the clique was happily knocking back the booze while they waited to eat. On the other hand I could see nobody from the band. I let out some invectives.

– Jesus fucking Christ, I'm not planning on playing hide and seek for the next week. Where the hell are these idiots?

Harry was much more fatalistic by nature.

– Calm down, that's not going to get them here. Since they left the Casino before us they should have been here by now. So it must be that de Brown wanted to drop by his hotel to change. Or something like that. So best to wait here a bit. If they're coming they'll be here within the next half hour. If they're not coming we know for sure we can get hold of them at the hotel. Aren't you a bit hungry anyway?

Harry was right and I knew it. But this little game of hide and seek was starting to drive me nuts.

I hated it even when I was little, and if I played hide and seek with other small fry of my age the first one I found hiding would get a fat lip. Which meant I got one too from my parents. Anyway, I was a bit peckish. Harry signalled to the *maître d'* and asked him to find us a table. We positioned ourselves so as to keep the Last Chance table conveniently in sight, which involved shifting a statue that was pointing a prophetic finger towards the restaurant door. Now she was pointing towards the johns, but the change would keep her from getting stiff.

I got a full translation of the menu. Even with the

translation none of the names of the dishes meant much to me. I settled for a dozen oysters and a rib of beef while Harry took a chance on *estouffade* of something or other and goose livers in aspic, like my chicken this morning. He went through the wine list like a connoisseur, dithered over it – we had all the time in the world – and plumped for a Château Whatchamacallit. I went for a cold beer. I'd just made up my mind to watch the booze intake, at least when I was on duty.

My tenth oyster was shivering under a spray of lemon when almost the entire band – only de Brown was missing – made its entrance. They weren't really in keeping with the tone of the restaurant, where you could count the bow ties and the evening dresses by the gross. They were greeted by a surprised silence, but they could hardly expect wild applause every time. It didn't bother them that much anyway. The performers weren't looking down in the mouth, which doesn't matter when you're in a restaurant. They were laughing a bit idiotically, slapping one another heartily on the back. They took a moment or two to spot the table where they were expected, and then their heartiness redoubled. Among the other patrons you could have heard a pin drop, which could have been fatal for the brasserie's reputation. But once the initial astonishment had passed, life won out again, as Duvall would one day write with reference to the international petition against the killing of whales and dolphins. The restaurant resumed its babble of noisy well-being and Harry joined in.

– Look at their table. There are still four reserved places. I wonder if they're coming.

He offered me a taste of his wine, but I've never liked the stuff much.

– I'm giving them another fifteen minutes Harry, then I'm beating it to the hotel. I really feel as if I've wasted a day.

– Relax, he soothed. You're not in New York now. Be like everybody here, take time out to live a little. It's not Dillinger you're tracking down, Sam.

– It doesn't matter who I'm tracking down Harry, it's the way I do it.

– I understand that, but don't worry, this case of yours isn't all that complicated.

When he said this he brought to mind the whole series of strange events before I left New York. The murder of the little drug dealer, the killers on the subway, the ransacking of my office, the gypsy's advice. On this side of the Atlantic it all seemed much quieter, and that's what amazed me. There was something in the air that I had no more than an inkling of, and I didn't like it at all. I didn't tell Harry. He'd heard too much stuff like that before. Without being able to say so I thought the opposite of him. The thought of it made my skin crawl. I gave nothing away and attacked my rib of beef listening with one ear to Harry's contented groans.

– How about it? This damned French cooking's really the tops.

I didn't share his enthusiasm. I'd ordered my meat well done and they'd brought it rare. I called over the first passing waiter and used Harry's skills as an interpreter to send both of them back to the kitchen. So I found myself waiting again. I don't think I've ever waited so much in my life as during that first day in Paris.

At that moment Turner made his entrance. He wasn't surprised to find us there and made do with a cautiously questioning look. 'They're not there!', our looks answered. He assumed a pained expression, gave a shrug of helplessness and moved away to the band's table. There were only three empty places left. And I couldn't see the use of roughing up Turner right now. The *maître d'* came back with my dog's dinner and an obsequious pout. I cut the meat open as he stood there. Blood poured out of it. It would have been better if I'd looked up my horoscope before putting a foot out the door this morning. I made an international gesture of refusal to the penguin, who hadn't stirred a fraction of an inch. Without hatred in my voice I said:

– MORE.

As he turned on his heels his left eyebrow looked like breaking loose, stirred no doubt by a nervous tic. This wasn't enough to spoil Harry's appetite; he was slaughtering his *estouffade* of something or other with a fatally aimed fork. Left to my own devices, I hazarded a glance at the Last Chance table. They weren't getting bored. Helped by the wine, the gathering had become thoroughly good-humoured. The musicians were exchanging anecdotes that produced bursts of raucous laughter. Only the journalists were showing restraint.

The rib of beef reappeared, this time brought by the chef in person. He came over to us, looking very displeased and with his chef's hat all askew. He stood right beside me and handed me the plate, muttering. He read out his proclamation:

– Sir, I am sorry. You are here in France, in a restaurant whose reputation is beyond reproach, and I refuse to treat food the way you do in your country. For I presume you're American.

108

He'd spoken as if we were two old perverts being nabbed by the vice squad.

– This is one of the best cuts of meat you could find in Paris, he said, indicating the slab of beef carcass, and I'm not the one who's going to permit the sacrilege of making it uneatable.

Harry gave me a succinct translation of the message. I slashed at the unfortunate steak just enough for it to spurt out several pints of scarlet blood. It was raw. I saw red. I was done to a turn. Quietly I got up from my chair, holding the dish under my nose, then I pushed it neatly under the chef's. I took the liberty of making him bend over until he was a quarter of an inch away from the meat, then I whispered in his ear, without bawling too loud:

– BURN IT!!!

My response left him speechless. He adjusted his hat, which I'd blown further sideways, lifted the plate in a hand as white as the collar round his neck, and turned towards his sanctuary. He was ready for sacrilege.

– A trip with you is an experience you should market with a travel agency. Let me tell you you'd make a fortune in no time. A sacrilege, huh . . . . Does he think the Bible's a cook book or what?

– Journeys are like a genesis, Harry.

We chortled at that.

Five minutes later I was brought a boot sole of sorts with a dash of contempt and some fries. I covered the whole thing in pepper to bring out the flavour and made short work of it. This time I'd waited long enough. We'd been there a good half hour and de Brown and Maria-Liza hadn't showed up yet. I glimpsed Turner heading down a stairway towards

109

the basement, in the direction of an illuminated sign that said 'Toilettes-Téléphone'. I gave him a couple of minutes, then I sneaked up behind him just as he was hanging up. What I mean is he'd been on the phone.

– I've just tried to reach them at the hotel, he said, forestalling me and simultaneously edging backwards, a tricky combination to get right. There's nobody there. I really can't think where they've gone. We're all waiting for them so as we can start eating.

– That's all right, I didn't bother waiting. Are you quite sure it's the hotel you called just now?

– I swear to you, Murchison, he insisted with as much conviction as he could muster.

– I've a gift for making people twitchy. I think if I put my mind to it I could irritate a statue of Buddha.

– Believe me, I'm as worried as you are, it's not like Joe. Or else he lets me know.

I felt there was nothing more I could get out of this loser. At least for now.

– Listen Turner, I'm staying at the Warwick too. You'll promise me something. You don't mind promising me something, do you?

– No, no, of course.

– I'm going back to the hotel. As soon as you get any news give me a call. Can I count on you?

– I promise you, Murchison, I'm starting to get really sick of this whole thing.

– Excellent, I'll be waiting.

I went back up to see Harry and told him what I'd decided. He didn't really mind, since he was planning to have a drink or two in a bar he said would bring back memories. I didn't want to know which ones. I had one of the waiters hail me a taxi then I propped a few bills on the table. Nobody tried to keep me.

– No kidding, Harry! We're citizens like everybody else here, don't forget it!

He raised his glass to me with a pickled smile. I left him with his nose in his Château.

ELEVEN

When I got to the Warwick I decided the only way to corner the two turtle doves if they weren't already in their room was to settle and wait for them out. The only snag in this terrifyingly shrewd plan was, of course, that I didn't know their room number. But that wasn't enough to stand in Sam Murchison's way. I noticed a teenager walking along the opposite sidewalk and waylaid him. I scribbled de Brown's name on a folded slip of paper – an invoice from the Tonkin' – and asked him, in a franglais that would make your hair stand on end, to hand it in at the hotel reception in exchange for a brand new bill. He hesitated slightly, then agreed outright, no questions asked, and pocketed the dough.

I fell into step behind him and mentally noted the number of the pigeonhole the receptionist put the note in. There were two keys in it, from which I concluded that there was nobody in the room. The kid made off without asking for his change. In any case there wasn't any.

Now I gave my number. No messages. I'd been put on the second floor while de Brown was on the sixth. I took the lift straight up there. The corridor was quiet and empty, and I had plenty of time to jiggle the lock with my magic rod. It gave in pretty soon.

If my suite was smart, theirs was sheer luxury. It must've run to something like ballroom size, perfect for golf practice. A vast sitting room with a terrace led on to a bedroom where you could have laid out a good dozen double mattresses. I inspected the premises to make sure there was really no one there. Deserted, but not empty. The place was heaped with an indescribable pile of junk. There were clothes everywhere, along with papers, records, bottles of Jim Beam, Canadian Club and champagne, panties, a few guitars, newspapers, half-unpacked suitcases, a huge tape deck, tapes, French and American currency, and thousands of different vitamin pills. The remains of a meal was ending its days on a vast marble table and a continuous blizzard pelted out of the television screen. They'd probably left it on for the sake of the snow. I made a cursory search. All the evidence showed that a male and a female were in residence. The wardrobe did for both sexes, and I loitered thoughtfully beside some underwear that anyone would have considered appetising. As for de Brown, he had a definite leather tendency. Leather with loads of metal things stuck all over it and sticking out at every angle. This stuff didn't leave him much chance of cutting any mustard with the Ninjas.

The newspapers were mostly French, and all of them were open at a page where someone wrote at length, at width and sometimes – in the case of the trendiest – diagonally, about the band. On the chest of drawers I spotted an itinerary for the week. It was Thursday today, and according to this the Last Chance were staying in Paris until Sunday, before leaving for Brussels, Rotterdam, Amsterdam, Zurich and London. I pocketed the itinerary and went on exploring. If I'd been in the shoes of the hotel management, I'd have immediately put in a small ad to sell off the bathroom. I really think even the skunk at Bronx zoo would have complained if they'd tried to put him in there. A variety of cosmetics stained the wash basin and the mirror, while something like a dozen strangely coloured towels lay on the floor sponging up the overflow from a bathtub nobody had thought needed to be emptied, probably out of respect for the animal life that would soon be spawn in it. I stepped over a few obstacles to take a closer look at the bathroom cabinet. A few bits of bloodstained cotton were in there, rolled into tiny balls. Not much to go on for a blood type. Someone round here had been bleeding from the nose or the arm. Ten bucks on the arm.

I went into the bedroom and found myself a spot where I could keep an eye on the door without the risk of being seen. It wasn't on purpose, but I ended up right next to the mini bar, which brought on a sudden thirst. The cupboard was pretty bare and the only thing I could rescue that was drinkable was a microscopic bottle of Canadian Club. Just enough for a consumer test, that was all. I did one, in a gulp. It was as if I'd drunk nothing, and in a fit of annoyance I sent the stunted little bottle flying across the room. All I could do was wait. The word was getting more and more on my nerves, but what can you do to a word? That's what I was trying to figure out when I dropped off. It was dead on 11.30 by my watch. The noise of the lock being turned brought me back to reality in a flash. I automatically looked at my watch again. 1.55. I could have sworn I hadn't closed an eye. It's little things like that that make you realise you're getting old.

I shrank back into the corner, ready to pounce. I

heard a few snatches of conversation coming from the sitting room. A man and a woman it seemed. But a distance I could only describe as considerable separated me from the door to the corridor, unless my hearing was playing tricks on me. I made plans for a complete check-up – another day – and crept towards the door to the sitting room.

I hazarded a sly peek and had the good fortune to catch the Belmont kid in my viewfinder. She was near the corridor door with her back to the wall, and was talking to someone I still couldn't see. I took time to check her out. The photo her father had given me was a long way off the original. She wasn't in brilliant shape, but on the other hand her shape was pretty brilliant. She must have been about five-foot-nine and classically proportioned in a way that would have made the ancient Greeks go gaga, and the young ones for that matter. Her statistics were something like 36-23-36, unless I was badly mistaken. This accuracy wasn't just a matter of my intimate knowledge of the female body. She was dressed in body-hugging clothes, which left no room for error. It would have taken a real old lecher to spot any, tiny as it might be. As for her face, somewhat heavy make-up wasn't enough to hide the kid's condition. Nothing wrong with her features, far from it, but you could see a kind of vacant look in the eyes that was made all the more pronounced by dark circles getting on for the size of a baseball diamond.

To my great surprise, Maria-Liza and her interlocutor – de Brown, undoubtedly – were talking about me. My arrival in Paris wasn't anything to enthuse about. She hadn't yet seen me in the flesh though. Put it this way, thanks to me she was developing a nice line in paranoia. De Brown was trying hard to reassure her,

115

saying there was no way I could get at her and that her father was entirely in the wrong.

– He thinks nothing stands in the way of his dough, but him and his asshole detective can't make you do anything you don't want to.

Asshole! He'd been given the wrong name. He went on:

– Relax, Liza, I'm going to run you a bath.

To run a bath there was no way he could avoid going into the bathroom. To get to the bathroom the only possible route went past me. So a second later I was face to face with him. The alarmed shriek he gave when he found me could have been fatal if he'd had a weak heart. I stood there silently, a gratified smile on my lips. The smile of the hunter who's getting close to the end of the trail and is relishing his triumph.

– Who . . . what . . . how . . . he stammered, who are you? What are you doing in this room?

He filled half the doorframe, and I was fast trying to move him so as not to lose sight of Maria-Liza, when I heard the door slam shut. She hadn't lost all her reflexes.

– Get the hell out of here, I screamed at de Brown, who did exactly the opposite and placed himself deliberately between me and the door. His reaction was so unexpected and things were happening so fast that the two of us ended up rolling on the floor, knocking over whatever stood in our path, which happened to be a single boot, also trying to find its match. I tried to jump to my feet, but de Brown was thinking ahead. Like a coward, he tripped me up and I charged head first into the door, which gave me the chance to test its solidity. It stood up well. But it wasn't enough to knock me out. For a few moments I saw the room going round and round then I came to as soon as I

116

stood up. I opened the door, with no hope left. The corridor had regained the calm that partly explained the price of the rooms. The lift wasn't moving, and the service stairs were as silent as an aquarium with no bubbles. All my rage came back again in the sitting room. De Brown, laid out on the carpet, hadn't stirred. I noticed a movement behind me, and, turning, identified it as Turner, half naked, coming to see what was up.

– What's going on, Christ, what's going on?

He realised when he saw me, and just stopped himself giving me a knowing grimace. I ignored him. It was only de Brown I was interested in. I wanted to kill him, but his reaction had been pretty normal, which was kind of an excuse.

– Get up kid, I told him, I'm not going to hurt you.

My attitude seemed to take him by surprise. He was in a perfect position for me to kick him in the mouth, and he was expecting something of the kind. But I'm not one for taking the easy way out. He stood up painfully and slumped onto the sofa without a word. Turner went and stood beside him as if he wanted to cover his frail shoulders with a protective wing. It was touching.

– Okay, I continued, here we are. You, de Brown, you must know all about the whys and the wherefores of me being here, if your tour manager has done his job properly. You, Turner, I've seen too much of you tonight, and you can beat it. Nothing I have to say to your charge here concerns you. Watch me, I'm closing my eyes, I'm counting to five, and you'll be gone.

I closed my eyes and counted to five.

– I'll try and see where she's gone, said Turner, in an attempt at a face-saving exit.

I heard the door slam.

– Quit throwing your weight around, Murchison, said de Brown, you'd think we were in a B movie. Why do you have to come along and mess things up for us like that, huh? Is it for the dough?

The youngster had a way with words.

– If you think your set-up's more like Ben Hur's, you're way off, de Brown. Sure I work mostly for dough, but I'm not the only one. So leave me out of it. I'll quit bugging you if you tell me why you're avoiding me like the big bad wolf.

– We're avoiding nobody, he answered smartly, we're being followed. It's not the same thing. Ever since Liza and I have been living together it's as if we'd murdered a VIP. No wonder we've had a bellyful.

– Nobody's got anything against you, de Brown. The kid's parents can't understand why she's stopped being in touch. Can't you get that into your head?

– She's had it up to here with her folks. She doesn't want to see them any more. Hell, what's so unusual about that? She's perfectly happy with me. Do I have the plague or something?

The two of us were moving along separate tracks, and yet I couldn't stop myself feeling sympathetic towards this kid. I didn't let it get to me.

– If she's so happy, how come she looks the way she does, and why can't she just make a phone call home? I can't see what would be out of the ordinary about that. And you'd have saved me the trouble of crossing the pond.

Suddenly his tone changed. As if he too was looking for an explanation.

– Listen, Murchison. I'll be honest with you, it'll save us some to-ing and fro-ing. Look, whether you like it or not, you see, I, the thing is, Liza, ever since . . . .

118

– You're up to your neck in drugs, I cut in.

He was face to face with a Sherlock Holmes looka-like. He was shattered.

– Oh! Who told you that?

– It would take a real putz not to see it. Have you looked in the mirror lately, apart from when you're lying down?

– Okay, okay. I won't try and lie to you. Anyway, I was getting to it. When I met Liza she'd never touched this kind of shit, except a bit of grass.

– Kids' stuff, huh, I remarked.

– That's it, kids' stuff. I think I made a big mistake turning her onto coke. She's totally hooked on it. She's started taking it in such a big way that I've got scared. But I was sure I'd make her see sense as time went by. You know what it's like when you discover something new.

– So that stops her from talking on the phone. Is that what you're telling me?

– No, it's not that. Let's say that it puts her more on edge than usual. And she's pretty nervy to start with; it doesn't help.

– How do you take your coke, tell me.

He gave me a condescending look.

– We sniff it, do you think it comes in suppositories or what?

– I've heard you can shoot it up too, and I didn't read that in *Cosmopolitan*.

– Oh no, that's only for addicts. Steer clear of that.

– I said nothing, I observed, setting him straight. Go on.

– That's about it. We're really gone on one another, she's giving her folks the cold shoulder and she's taking too much coke. There's your story, good huh?

119

– It may be good for Barbara Walters. It's not good enough for me. If you really think she's taking too much coke all you have to do is quit giving it to her. She's hardly known you two weeks, it's not enough time to get hooked on that shit. Are you sure you've told me everything?

He looked like he wanted to leave. I blocked the way out.

– You know everybody goes in for coke in this business. It's always around whichever way you look. I'm not the one who gives it to her, it's another musician. I can't be watching out for her all the time.

I knew that wasn't enough to make him want to run.

– Answer my question, kid.

– Yeah, okay, sometimes we take a bit of . . . .

This was the moment Turner chose to come beating on the door to be let in. I went to open it.

– Vanished! I've been round all the rooms, the stairs, the lobby, nobody's seen her. This thing's really crazy. What's with her?

– Leave it, de Brown soothed him, she'll come back. Go to bed. I'll wait up for her.

He didn't need to be told twice.

– Ring me if there's any problem at all, Joe. So long, Murchison.

He vanished again.

– You were saying? I came back at de Brown.

– Yeah, sometimes we take a little smack too. But nothing serious, just a sniff.

– So there we are! You see, you could do it. Otherwise apart from that everything's okay?

He didn't really grasp what I meant by that. I went and sat beside him.

120

– Find something to drink in this dump, we'll wait for her together.

I took out my Winstons.

– Do you smoke?

TWELVE

There was time to finish my pack of cigarettes and a reserve bottle of Jack Daniels that de Brown kept in a closet. In fact, we spent the whole night, no less, stuck on that cursed sofa chewing the fat. He wasn't a bad guy at all. The booze loosened his tongue and the lines of coke he snorted at regular intervals made it too nervous to relax. I pretended not to notice each time he bent over the low marble table to shake out his little piles of powder and cut them in lines. It was nice to watch but it drew another line between the two of us that was impossible to cross. He even went so far as to offer me some. I declined. I thought I was being cool enough already not to have dissolved his stash in the bathtub. He didn't press me.

He was a real kid. I reckoned about twenty with a good lawyer, and he admitted he'd just celebrated his twentieth birthday. It would have been risking too much to bet on him making it to forty at this clip, but in a way it was understandable. Until he was eighteen he'd known nothing about life outside Long Island, where his family lived. His father drove a school bus, and his mother cleaned up in an old people's home. No money, not much hope of having more in the future; the only two things he really cared about were football and music. He'd worked out pretty fast that the former wasn't for him, unless he got himself a different body and a few dozen pounds of muscles. So he'd taken the soft option and watched football on TV like everybody else. The only hitch was that after six months touring his ass off, and the odd flash in the pan, things had really taken off in Europe, and were a lot less hot on the east coast of the US. Within eighteen months he was living a Cinderella lifestyle twenty-four hours a day without any pumpkin at midnight. He hadn't spent too much time in class at high school, but it hadn't stopped him from moving straight up the class divide. And everything suggested success for the rest of his life. He was welcomed everywhere like a prince, the record industry en masse waxed poetic about his talent and genius, and he couldn't take a walk without signing a heap of autographs. I don't know many people who could deal with this kind of treatment. His way of entering the whirlwind and living through all the clichés strewn in his path lay in ingesting everything within reach through his mouth, his nose, and, I was convinced, his veins pretty soon. If he had music in his blood it would have company before long. He was taking refuge in a lifestyle the way other people do in a religion. Things had gone so far that it wouldn't have done any good telling him how bad they were. He didn't give a damn about burning himself out, and he reminded me of a Belgian mercenary I'd come across a few years earlier. Likewise he wasn't looking to live long, he only wanted it to be intense. I had nothing against this, quite the opposite, but de Brown's way made my hair stand on end. He thought he was controlling his life, but he was the one being controlled. While I was telling myself this I realised fatigue had me getting all tangential. I'd have to be fried to be thinking this doomsday stuff. I yawned and pulled myself together, catching the drift of Joe's story, which was well under way.

He'd got to the bit where he'd met Maria-Liza during a stop in Miami. I wasn't spared the earth-shattering love-at-first-sight stuff, nor the 'she's so different from all the others', nor 'it's the real thing between us'. Along with fame and fortune he had the third accessory: girls. He told me there'd been an endless procession until he met HER. From that moment on, the rest of womankind had disappeared from his reality. The first day she'd claimed never to have heard of the the Last Chance, and money was something she couldn't use. No, it was different, and God, he'd never imagined getting into a state like that over a broad. He said in her eyes every single thing he did was thrilling and wonderful and you name it. He could have asked her to jump off the Washington Bridge into the Hudson and she'd have done it dou-ble-time, even anticipating the request. He had to be careful about what he said. Deep down it scared him a bit, what he called 'a passion like this'.

I was listening to this appalling story with only half an ear when he started talking about the Belmont parents. Maria-Liza had spent her life wrapped in cottonwool. Protected from everything, with no fears for the future, in a sanitised comfort where everything ran too smoothly. In exchange for this Mummy and Daddy demanded an almost blind submission. I was familiar with this kind of story. Then one fine day, fatally, along comes the 'mischief-maker' and all the best laid plans come to nothing, or might as well have. Would she get back on the straight and narrow? In cases like this you have to wait a bit for the answer, but

124

it's usually affirmative in the end. Here, we were in the dark. The fragile blue blossom had changed overnight, and she would no longer obey. Even to the point of refusing any contact at all. And on their side, there was the wringing of hands, the weeping and wailing, the reminders about father's weak heart. All in vain. She didn't want to hear another thing about them; with de Brown she'd discovered love and the delights of escape. I could imagine the romantic yarn a new Barbara Cartland could have concocted from it. But in my version of the story, a new element complicated things: drugs.

– It's nothing to worry about, Murchison. We're only having fun with them. We take them just for kicks, to blank out some of the pressure I'm under. But we're not addicts thinking of scoring from morning till night. It's true it's wearing her out a bit but I'm going to cut her off soon. Anyway I've had enough, and so long as it's for her, nothing else matters.

I pulled him up short before he could get going again on the great love theme. Time had flown, it was getting on for 6 a.m.

– Listen, son, maybe I'm barking up the wrong tree, but even though I can't put my finger on it, I've a hunch there's something funny going on. I'm not saying you're mixed up in it. I'm even convinced you're not. But you realise there's a lot of dough washing around you. To tell you the truth, there are people I don't know who're doing everything they can to stop me getting near Liza. Don't ask me why, I haven't a clue. But it'll come to me. Okay, you're in your little bubble, you can do what you like inside it, I don't care. The only thing that matters to me is her. As soon as she's calmed down send her to me. I'll telephone her father, she'll say whatever she wants to him, just one word if she likes, but she'll open her mouth and talk. From then on I'll have done my job, I'll leave you in peace and I'll sort out my business like a big boy. Is that okay?

It was fine and dandy.

– Okay, we'll come and see you as soon as she gets back. What's your room number?

– 201. I'm going to flop for a bit, I'm bushed. I'll wait to hear from you. And get some rest, you wouldn't be fit for a sanatorium.

– Sure, sure, okay, don't worry, I'm not going anywhere.

I had trouble imagining him dropping off to sleep with all that stuff up his nose. He was ready to do a few hours flying, or do a handstand on the ceiling, exercise anyhow. As for me, I perked up once I got moving. The blood started circulating in my legs again, easing the tiredness. I called the lift and asked it to take me down gently. There was an undisturbed, soothing calmness that made me poetic about hitting the sack. I got my key out and unlocked the door. I had scarcely opened it a fraction when a muffled sound, like something rubbing against soft fabric, told me someone was waiting for me – I've no idea why this sound alerted me; probably an old reflex. And at that hour they certainly weren't waiting to take me for a run in the woods. I automatically flung my whole weight on the door and pushed it back against the wall. I dived into the sitting room bent double, and in the darkness collided with my own low table, which was also of the marble variety. But there wasn't much damage done and, just as I was getting up, light flooded the room. There were two of them. Armed. Either side of the door. The one who'd chosen the bad side was wriggling on his knees, shielding his face.

126

The other one though was looking round for his target, dazed by the speed of what had just happened.

His target was me. Without giving him the time to adjust his sights I covered the two yards between us in less time than Buster Keaton would have taken not to smile (RIP). I relieved him of his weapon with a splendid tobi-keri and followed up with a mae-geri well to the temple. In the same movement I pivoted round and landed a super mawashi-geri in the other guy's guts. They were now both on their knees, just like most of the furniture, but I didn't let it get to me. The first thing I did was grab the two guns and fling them across the sitting room. I quickly turned back to my first victim, picking him up and hurling him against the wall, since that seemed to be one of his favourite spots. That was my first mistake. I was trying to revive him a little when I got hit on the back by one of the solid wood easy chairs. A stabbing pain shot right through me and I fell on my knees, without passing out. I was aware that the one who'd just let me have it was pulling his buddy by the arm and I heard them hightailing it to the service stair. I put all my strength into kicking the door shut, and made a superhuman effort to fasten the chain. After dealing with these tiny details, I collapsed onto the rug again and succumbed wholeheartedly to the buffalo charge that was running and re-running over my spine. For a while I gave myself over to the almost unbearable pain, savouring every twinge. Gradually, I was able to move a little, just enough to check nothing was broken or dislocated. I was okay; the sitting room, though, had it had the power of speech, would have said something different. It looked like demolition night at the Warwick. I took about five minutes to get up, using some breathing and self-relaxation techniques. I had something real special in mind for the two thugs; they'd better make the most of life before they crossed me again.

I made a pit stop in the bathroom to splash my face with cold water and remembered the guns. As expected, they were still there. I picked them up with my handkerchief and without hoping for too much. I couldn't see the French cops doing any lab tests just for the sake of my sanity, and Harry couldn't do much this end. They were nice pieces, Italian and American. On my left, a Beretta 90 automatic, on my right, a Ruger Security Six Magnum 357. On the other hand, since the little skirmish had transpired without a word, there was nothing to tell me the nationality of my hitmen. All the same I was inclined to go for Yanks. You come across Berettas all over the place, but Rugers are made in Connecticut, and they seldom cross frontiers. This one, manufactured some time after 1970, was hardly a collector's item, but I didn't think it travelled in bulk. I'd check that out with Harry, later. I put the shooters down on the famous marble table, which had valiantly resisted my attack, and got undressed as delicately as possible. My back, it turned out, was marbled too, black and blue. I ran the water and let myself down – just this once – into a scalding hot bath, carefully and splashily. The heat was immediately soothing, and I could easily have fallen asleep if I'd let myself. Then I found a pack of Excedrin in my bag and gulped down three. It worked miracles. There and then, I hit the hay and let myself be carried away on a tidal wave of exhaustion.

THIRTEEN

As usual it was the telephone that woke me. De Brown was on the line, to coin a phrase, letting me know that Maria-Liza had finally come back. He told me she'd spent the rest of the night wandering around Paris not wanting to talk to anyone, and that she was literally dropping from exhaustion. But he'd put her in the picture and she'd agreed to see me for five minutes to make him happy. My back was hurting a lot less, but I took three more Excedrin to kill the pain completely. It was 8.45 on the alarm clock and I'd happily have slept another week. I put on the same clothes as before and left the room with circumspection, an old buddy of mine. They'd been waiting for me inside, so they could just as easily wait for me outside. There was no one in sight except a cleaning woman who watched me advance one door at a time towards the lift as if I was playing cat and canary.

– It's a forfeit, I told her, I've lost playing a silly game, it's just a forfeit.

She understood English like I understood Bantu, and she went on looking more stupefied than amused until I'd disappeared into the elevator.

De Brown opened the door to me. He looked even

worse than he had three hours earlier, but better than he would the following evening if he went on missing sleep. I saw Liza huddled in a corner of the sofa. I walked in past Joe and he made introductions. I avoided any gags about our first, informal meeting and sat down opposite her in an armchair almost as wide as the hotel's entrance. My being there didn't seem to cut much ice with her, and she tossed me a chilly hello without taking her gaze off the pattern on the Persian rug as she chomped a chunk of chewing gum. She'd flung her jacket aside, into the middle of the room, but it wasn't on its own, having met up with five or six pairs of pants that it knew well. As I was about to speak to her, as gently as I could, she spat her gum onto an unsuspecting boot.

– Mr Murchison, she said, still staring at the floor – I wondered if it wouldn't look better for me to place myself in her line of vision – I know why my father sent you here, but I don't want to see him, or hear from him, or . . . .

She burst into sobs. When it came to crazies, this was the best I'd seen for a long time. De Brown held her tenderly and told her to calm down, that everything would be fine, that I was an okay guy, and so on. She snivelled and sniffed for a while, which was something they did a lot of round here, then finally looked me straight in the eyes. I like seeing women weep, it makes them more human and clear-eyed. But these eyes didn't need tears. Her eyes were neither hard nor tear-dimmed, but limpid and troubled. She carried her tiredness wonderfully. I weighed in.

– Maria-Liza, what's going on between you and your family isn't my business, and I've no intention of kidnapping you to return you to the fold. I'm being paid to find you and make sure everything's okay. It'll all be much simpler if you have a word with your father on the phone.

– No!

She didn't want to.

I glanced at de Brown to see his reaction and he speedily took the hint.

– Listen, cherub – no wonder he'd snuggled her under his wing – it's no big deal. Just say two words to him and they'll all leave us in peace. If you won't do it for him, do it for me. We can't go on being hounded like this week after week.

– Don't want to.

She still didn't want to. I switched gear.

– We'll leave that till later. That's the first part of my contract. The second, as I've just said, is to make sure everything's okay. It isn't, is it?

That really got to her.

– What's with everyone that you're all spying on me? I can't move any more without being asked where I'm going, who with, as if I was going to commit a murder. I'm going to end up . . . .

– Calm down, Liza, urged de Brown.

– Calm down, Liza, calm down, Liza, that's all you can say, calm down, Liza.

When it came to great love stories, I'd seen better. I decided to call a halt to this domestic psychodrama.

– That's enough you two, you're starting to really get me down. I didn't come three thousand miles to play nursemaid. Maria Liza, I'll give you the whole day to get back on your feet, then at 6 on the dot you're going to speak to your father on the phone. If that doesn't suit you, I'm locking you in the bathroom, in the water or under the water, whichever, until you agree.

I felt as if I was scolding two naughty little children.

131

That was exactly it. Maria-Liza looked at me with thoroughly startled eyes, and de Brown shut up. I decided to leave things there without digging into the drug stuff at all. There was nothing to be lost by waiting. It could get the full-scale interrogation treatment this evening. I got up, leaving them with these words:

– No fooling, Liza, otherwise I'll really get mad.

I'd thought I'd have a handle on what was going on by the end of the day. The band was playing at the same place, as I'd seen on the schedule. Okay! If this evening wasn't enough, I still had the whole of the next day, when they were doing interviews. It would be just one more for them. I made my way back to my room, on my guard, but without running into the cleaning woman. I couldn't have because she was there cleaning my suite. But she wasn't armed. My bit of territory sure was a thoroughfare. After thinking she'd seen one of the hotel rats, she was now in an elephant's bedroom. Well, after an elephant had dropped by . . . . Her look of amazement soon reappeared when she saw me come in. I made it clear everything was fine and there was nothing I needed. I went with her as far as the corridor and locked the door behind her, remembering to hang out the 'Do Not Disturb' sign. Sometimes my sense of humour really swings.

My back was back. I got undressed again and this time gave a groan of satisfaction as I took a dive onto the bed. I called reception to have a six-egg omelette sent up with fried potatoes. My fridge was packed solid with beer. I hung on to the phone and dialled international. Seconds later a phone was ringing in Miami. It was 3.30 in the afternoon there and there was a chance I'd catch Belmont at home. I got his wife.

I had the family coming out of my ears but it didn't hurt too much. My call was expected.

– Well? she asked, no preliminaries.

– Well fine, I lied. I've found Liza. I don't know what you did to her, but it looks like out and out rebellion. I've persuaded her to talk to you later today. But I can't see her going back home to you tomorrow.

– My little girl, my poor little girl, she started sobbing.

I turned off the waterworks.

– Mrs Belmont, there's no big crisis here. She's run away from home like hundreds do every day, and things will settle down if you give them some time. Listen, your husband sent me here so I could get Maria-Liza to a phone and he could hear the sound of her voice. That'll happen this evening. Stay close to your phone around 2 a.m.

– Yes, okay, 2 a.m. Mr Murchison, I know my husband desperately wanted to talk to you. I'll get him at his office and tell him to call you back now.

– Very well, ma'am, speak to you later.

I hung up cursing the name Belmont. But that's the way it goes with 99 per cent of people when they think of their employer.

I woke up Harry. He told me, hemming and hawing, that he'd met an old girlfriend who was a dancer and they'd spent most of the night dancing; appropriately. Anyway, she was still here – but . . . no, wait, if . . . – she was still asleep. I got the message and gave him back his freedom.

– Call me back when you're awake, okay?

– Fine, Sam, when you wake up. *Ciao, bello.*

Thee was a knock at the door. This room had to be the liveliest spot in the hotel. I put on a dressing gown and checked through the spyhole. I saw my omelette,

133

brought by the same floor waiter as the day before. When he saw the battlefield he couldn't hold back a little whistle. I kept him happy with another tip and sent him off without a word. I checked the security chain and the two locks and took my tray over to the bed with a little whistle of my own. I was just about to shovel in the first mouthful when the phone started ringing. It was Belmont, all nerves.

– Mr Murchison, I'm delighted you've found Maria-Liza. How is she?

– Not too bad, I lied again. But there's no question of her . . . .

– I know, he interrupted. My wife explained.

That would save some breath.

– Listen, I won't beat around the bush. Life isn't worth living for my wife with Maria-Liza so far away and acting so sore with us.

He was still sprouting some real humdingers. He must have had a gardenful by now.

– There's 5,000 dollars in it for you if you bring her back to us.

– Hey there! I exclaimed. Let me remind you your daughter isn't a minor.

– I know, I know, Mr Murchison, but she needs to see sense. I've already told you, she's still a child and as soon as she's back here she'll forget this whole sorry episode very quickly.

If you wanted to give space to a whole brood of kids like that it was fine by me.

– I'm not sure you're right, Mr Belmont. But be patient and trust me, I'll do my best to persuade her.

He didn't see things like that.

– Maybe you misheard me? I WANT, he said tersely, you to bring Maria-Liza back home, however you do

134

it. I'm offering you 5,000 dollars for that. Am I making myself understood?

For no apparent reason, I sensed there was something fishy going on.

– Give me the rest of the day, I'll let you have my answer tonight. 2 a.m.

– Agreed, but I'm counting on you Murchison, we'll speak tonight.

I hung up and attacked my omelette, while I tried to make sense of the whole shemozzle. This guy was rolling in it. His darling daughter, who'd reached the age of consent, had consented with a musician, and hadn't got back in touch. Griefstricken mother. He decides to hire one of the best detectives on the east coast to find her. He finds her. She doesn't want to see her folks again, he offers me a nice round sum to bring her back at all costs.

Meanwhile, I'm sent threats via a third party, there's an execution as soon as I try to talk to somebody, and I'm the target for a hit in New York and Paris too. And there's snow falling everywhere on top of it, despite Christmas being a long way off. Who, how and why? I asked myself. But I was out of answers. The whole thing smelled like a barrelful of rotten fish. I was being used like a dice and I didn't know what board they were rolling me on. To put it another way, I could be on a losing streak.

The phone rang again. Cardier.

– Go to hell, I told him politely. I'm not opening my mouth again until tonight.

I hung up again and immediately contradicted myself by opening a beer. My bed was waiting, ready. I didn't resist.

FOURTEEN

I was in the middle of a dream about a world without telephones when a ringing sound pierced my eardrums. Harry was on the line in a lather.

– What are you up to, dammit, you sleeping or what? At 4 in the afternoon!

I could hardly believe I'd snoozed away all that time, but I didn't feel guilty about it. As everyone knows, when you're asleep you don't notice time go by.

– Weren't you meant to call me between 11.30 and 12? I asked him after stopping to think about it.

– Nah! It was you that should've woke me.

This could have gone on for a long time.

– Mind you, he went on, I'm not holding it against you. Take my word for it, I haven't been wasting my time waiting for you.

– You've been going round the museums? I ventured.

– The temple of pleasure, old man, yeah, the temple of pleasure.

I remembered his dancer.

– Come and say hello to the temple doorkeeper. I've got a few things I want to ask you.

He said he was on his way and, sure enough, moments later there was a knock on my door. Through the spyhole I saw a terribly distorted Harry, but it kinda suited him. He was in dazzling form. His first words were for the sitting room.

– Wow! Did you lose something or have you taken up carpentry? was the crack he came up with.

The chest of drawers, the desk, the little writing table and the low table were overturned, and the drawers had wandered all over the place.

– I've had visitors. And they weren't Jehovah's Witnesses, as you can see. They tried to skin me alive again last night.

That floored him.

– What? Even here in Paris? Hey, going to have to get yourself an armoured car to go around in, if you want to live. Do you know your 'visitors'?

– They forgot to leave me their card. They forgot those too, I said, pointing to the guns.

He approached them with the self-conscious air of an expert, and gave them the once-over.

– Beretta and Ruger. The Beretta was first made in '66 in Brescia, Italy, and it's still being manufactured. It sells pretty well. The Ruger in 1970, back home, but it's much less widely used, except by the cops.

This was his walking encyclopaedia side. I suddenly remembered the cleaning woman, but she couldn't have noticed anything. She wouldn't have left the room with so little fuss.

– Can you do anything about tracking down the owners? I asked him, not very optimistically. I'd like to see them again soon.

He thought a while then came up with two suggestions. In the first place he could take down the serial numbers and have them checked out by his depart-

ment to see if they featured on the lists. And then of
course he could also ask Interpol to check the prints.
But I wasn't wild about the idea. I've never believed in
too many cooks.

– Try New York, and forget Interpol. I'd rather keep
it in the family.

One of Harry's great virtues was his discretion. He
seized hold of the weapons, since we were going to
forget about the prints, and took down the numbers
on a piece of paper. He did all this without a word of
argument. Then he came over to the phone.

– It'll take about an hour. Can I use your phone?

– Make yourself at home. Your vacation's not
exactly getting off to a flying start, is it?

– Hogwash. If I've got nothing to do I get pissed off.

I was kind of an ideal partner for him. I took the
trouble to explain what had happened the night
before, though without explaining why, which I
didn't know anyway. But Harry was clever enough to
piece things together for himself. All the same I told
him about the 5,000.

– You should forget it, he said in total seriousness. It
could cost you a lot more than you'd make from it.

He was 100 per cent right, and I had no intention of
getting mixed up in this kind of imbroglio. Daddy
Belmont was going too far, losing his sense of reality. I
put it down to an overdose of dollars.

– Guys like that think all they have to do is snap
their fingers and they can run people's lives. I can see
why the kid's run out on them. And how would he
like you to bring her back? Tied up in a trunk or what?
Tell me I'm dreaming.

– What he really wants is for me to persuade her. At
any price.

No way was I going along with any of it.

138

– Listen Sam, you're to see the Belmont kid at 6, isn't that right? It'll be an hour before I have an answer from New York. What if we went out and took a little stroll around? You've got to see Paris after all, it's a must.

– Okay, let's go and have a drink, but we'll stay in the neighbourhood. I'm not up to seeing old sights.

– Ninety per cent of the bars in this neighbourhood are old sights. People here spend more time in them than they do in bed, take my word for it.

I had a quick wash and got dressed in no time. The Champs-Elysées was thronged with people. A massive traffic jam was blocking the avenue, under a leaden sky. Car horns were hooting in every direction, making a shocking din. I was amazed that so much noise could come from such tiny cars. I thought about it.

– It's like mutts, I observed, the smaller they are, the more they yap.

Even if it was overpopulated this neighbourhood did have style. It was the first avenue of a decent width I'd seen since I arrived. Harry dragged me as far as Fouquet's and insisted we sit at one of the sidewalk tables. It meant he could keep a tally of the talent that went by. He went into fits about every last one of them, finding each new female even more attractive than the one before. True, the overall effect was pretty impressive. I counted very few in baggy jeans or jogging outfits, as is often sadly the case States-side. But I wasn't quite up to making in-depth comparisons, and I sipped my Marguerita unperturbed. Harry talked away on his own, passing remarks and giving a running commentary on faces and figures. His Guinea blood was getting good and hot. Now that he was a lot closer to the old country it has to be said it was getting to him. Around the twelve thousandth victim I looked at my watch and saw it was already 5.20.

– The session's over Harry, duty calls, for you too.

I paid for our drinks and left a hefty tip. You should always bring gifts when you make the acquaintance of foreign peoples. I bought the only American newspaper they had in the kiosk opposite the café – the *Herald Tribune* – and we went back across the avenue towards the hotel. Just as it began to drizzle.

We struck out with the serial numbers. The weapons had already been out of circulation for a good while, as was to be expected. Since their legit purchase nobody had filed a complaint until now. I'd have been surprised if that wasn't the case. I told Harry my plans for the evening: to stay with Maria-Liza and not take my eyes off her for a moment. That meant I was in for another concert. Harry had far more exciting things in mind and he looked let down. He made up his mind to go it alone, or rather alone with a young lady of his acquaintance. This guy wasn't so much an address book, more a telephone directory. He found a good restaurant where he could ruin his stomach and gave me the address in case I changed my mind later.

– I'll be there between 9 and 11. Afterwards though, I'll be going my own sweet way. I'm on vacation, you know, he said as if by way of reproach.

After some closing remarks on what the city had to offer he left me to it. He was a good guy when all was said and done. I wasn't long in following behind. I put the 'Do Not Disturb' sign back on my door. When I closed it I used a trick any detective story fan would have pulled me up on. I slipped a piece of cellophane torn from my cigarette packet under the door a fraction. If anybody entered, the draught alone would be enough to dislodge it. I headed back up to the sixth floor; I could have got there with my eyes shut, but it wouldn't have been practical. At 5.55 precisely I reached de Brown's suite. It was Maria-Liza who opened the door to me in a bath robe. I could imagine Harry going red as a beet with this package in front of him, wrapped up this way. Thinking of him cued my own self-control. She seemed in better shape than that morning, and she even went as far as to give me a smile. I checked I hadn't got the wrong room and went inside, amazed.

– Joe's gone to the Casino, Mr Murchison, he wanted to check the mix. He wasn't happy with it yesterday. Sit down, make yourself at home.

I saw things were still pretty much in the same mess, but a few things had been moved around during the day. It looked like Saks just after the sales. I sat in the same armchair and Liza settled onto the same spot, on the sofa. She'd come out of the shower. She'd piled her long hair into a giant towel that became a turban. She was delicious.

– Well, are you ready, Liza?

– Yeah, okay, don't worry about me. I'll talk to him, she said, giving her arm a sharp little scratch – vulgar, but a nail's still nicer than a needle.

I lifted the phone and made it ring five thousand miles away. It was answered at once. Daddy Belmont.

– Murchison speaking. Please hold, I've got your daughter for you.

I gave Liza the phone. She started talking to him the way you answer a Bowery wino who's trying to hit you for a quarter. She would have sounded the same if she'd never met the guy at the other end of the phone. She told him everything was fine.

– Why've I done this? Why've I done that? I've got

141

nothing to say to you. I'm grown up now, you can't tell me anything.

– . . . .

She got a bit madder. Anger suited her.

– Because I felt like it, that's all. Anyway, there was no point in asking you, you'd have said . . . .

– . . . .

– No, I don't want to go home, I'M NOT GOING HOME . . . . I want to live my own life, I've had enough of people telling me to do things I . . . .

– . . . .

– NO, I'M NOT GOING HOME . . . .There's no point in insisting, otherwise you'll never hear from me again . . . I don't want to . . . . Hello, hello, Mummy . . . .

– . . . .

– Listen, Mummy, don't get all upset. It's not you I'm angry with, it's . . . .

– . . . .

– Mummy, stop it, it's no good, STOP IT . . . STOP IT . . . . She flung down the phone, jumped up and ran and locked herself in the bathroom, slamming the door. I grabbed the phone and made sure we hadn't been cut off.

At the other end of the line all you could hear was shouting. Mummy was wailing while Daddy was swearing like a trooper: 'Little bitch, little bastard – whore, etc.', which didn't show much delicacy towards his wife. I waited for things to calm down a bit, then I gave a cough the way one does to draw attention. I was very quickly noticed.

– Murchison, roared Belmont, are you still there? I WANT you to bring her back tomorrow on the first plane, is that clear?

I didn't want to, but I didn't feel like saying no, at

least not at that particular moment. I wasn't in the mood to argue with a madman, even with an ocean between us. Maria-Liza was sobbing in the next room and I felt more like looking after her.

– I'll call you back later, Mr Belmont, leave it to me.

I hung up without waiting for his answer. I went over and crouched down by the door, doing my best to calm the creature quaking on the other side.

– Come on, Liza, it's all over, I put the phone down. Calm down. Come out here.

– No, leave me alone, I want to be alone. I'm sick of it all, came the snub.

– Okay, do what you like. I'll wait for you in the sitting room. When you feel better come out.

There was no answer. It occurred to me that she might just do something silly, but I convinced myself she wouldn't. I'd known people really at their wits' end. She still had wits to spare. I made myself comfortable again, this time on the sofa, after divesting the fridge, which had happily been refilled, of some whisky and soda. I made myself a jaunty little cocktail and switched on the TV. There's nothing like background noise to calm the nerves. I couldn't make out a word of what they were saying, but I wasn't missing much. It was a documentary about short-haired poodles. There was a guy using illustrations to explain their reproductive life, which was very like our own, their diet, diseases and death. There were tearful old biddies remembering their dear departed Theos and Fifis, next to the graves where these molly-coddled monstrosities were resting for all eternity. I wondered whether they still hadn't invented pest control in France, and tried another channel. That was even easier to understand. Two guys were looking at scrambled letters of the alphabet and putting them in

143

the right order, while a third guy was handing them out, looking as if it was the happiest day of his life. Maybe he'd lost his poodle on the way there. I got the momentary impression that I'd ended up on another planet, but I thought better of it when I remembered the dreck on the tube back home. I gave up on the small screen and took a look through my paper. Nothing much had happened in the world while I'd been asleep.

Fifteen minutes had trickled away, and the bath too, going by the noise, when I heard the lock turn. The door was opened gingerly and Maria-Liza appeared, looking somewhat drawn. Her turban was gone and her mane of damp hair tumbled round her face in a tangle. She was staggering a little as she came and sat beside me without saying a word. There was something pitiful about her. I took her by the chin and looked at her. I was alone. The eyes across from mine had been temporarily vacated. I settled her down as comfortably as I could, then got up and went across to the bathroom. There I found a small syringe that she hadn't even bothered to hide, and a belt that must have done duty as a tourniquet. I punched my fist furiously against the wash basin and let out a howl. Things were getting serious. I didn't feel like laughing now.

FIFTEEN

I was considerably less delicate with the poor little rich bird from the golden cage. I took hold of her, this time by the shoulder, and shook her like a broken-down slot machine, which is exactly what she was. But I hit the jackpot, and she started shouting for help. I slapped her half a dozen times, which calmed her down a bit and gave her a bit of colour. This whole commotion had made her bathrobe slip down and her breasts were exposed. I gulped at the sight of so much perfection, then tidied her up. I sure picked a dumb way to earn a living. I dumped her brusquely on the sofa. She collapsed with her legs under her. It reminded me of Bambi. So much for hearts and flowers. I've always hated Walt Disney. Especially Pluto. I sat down on the armrest and got started.

– Playtime's over, honey, homework's due in now. Who's the big baddie who gives you this nose candy, huh, who is it, tell me, hurry up.

– Why so much hatred? she sighed.

You'd have thought we were back in the seventies. I always hated the seventies.

– We're all brothers and sisters, my darling. So tell your big brother. Who's the shit who gets you high?

145

Out with it, I'm getting bored.

She shot up and headed for the bathroom. This time I beat her to it and blocked the doorway. It wasn't that she wanted to lock herself in. What she had in mind was a little face to face with the toilet. It wasn't a pretty sight. I can't think of anything more dismal than a beautiful girl throwing up. I averted my eyes discreetly. When she had prised herself out I put my arm round her and took her back to the sitting room. I almost felt sorry for her. It's better to avoid that kind of thing.

– I feel better, she said, with a shy smile.

She could hardly have felt any worse.

– Then talk to me, tell me everything.

– But why do you want to know? It's got nothing to do with you, has it?

She was gradually coming back to life. If you can call pupils dilated like pinpoints life.

– I have my reasons, I replied, shaking her a bit more.

– Stop it, stop it. It's the guys in the band who give me the stuff, but you won't say anything to them, will you?

It was starting to come out, though de Brown had said more or less the same thing last night. But I was getting more and more interested. Fascinated even.

– Fine. You're going to get dressed, make yourself look nice, then we're both going to the concert. Put on your make-up, you could do with it, you look about thirty right now.

I was scarcely exaggerating, she was in a ghastly state. She was surprisingly compliant; casually, she started picking up a few rags that had been lying on the floor. It didn't bother her getting dressed in front of me, but I preferred not to look. I don't like voyeurs,

146

at least not in this kind of situation. She went back to the bathroom and I stuck behind her. I had no more time to play hide and seek, but I think she'd lost the desire. While she was doing her repair job she gabbled on about life in general, without me paying much attention. In no time she was presentable again. We'd got acquainted. She was even talking about getting me a permanent pass for the whole tour. But I wasn't reckoning on following the band much longer. I watched her out of the corner of my eye as I got on the blower to call a taxi. She cut me short, saying de Brown always left a limousine at her disposal. Probably to keep her in the style to which she was accustomed. So we went straight to the garage where a huge Mercedes was waiting with a driver. Maria-Liza looked a bit like she was floating. All her movements were slow and she'd turned off the chatter. I told the driver where we were headed, but he knew already. His charabanc was the lap of luxury. There was an old calypso coming out of the radio and I could feel my good humour gradually resurfacing.

During the whole ride not a word passed between us. Liza watched the streets go by through the window and I watched Liza watch the streets go by. Through the window. I couldn't get over what a mess she was in. A bit like a vegetable – unaware it would end up in the smooth hands of a vegetarian some day. It seemed unnatural to go in for so much self-destruction. The driver was minding his own business. He was humming quietly along with the music, taking no notice of us. I lit up a Winston. It roused Liza and she asked me for one.

– How are you feeling, kid?

Eighty per cent of the questions a man asks in his lifetime are stupid.

– Fine, fine, there's nothing for you to worry about, I'm feeling really great, she said, giving me a blank look.

I sank back into the musical silence. It was still raining. I was just going to stub out my cigarette when we reached the Casino. It was all just the same as the night before, so exactly the same that I wondered whether I hadn't entered a time warp. But that hardly ever happens except in films, and usually bad ones.

I got out of the car on the same side as Liza and we went to the stage door, avoiding the crowd that was pushing at the door. The gonzo bouncer recognised me. He was just about to bare his teeth when I showed off my pass. I think he'd really have loved to make me eat it, metal tag and all, and not necessarily by way of mouth. We went down a long corridor before we got right backstage. People were rushing around all over the place. We came across Turner talking into the phone. He looked at me as if he'd seen a ghost.

– Murchison, just the man . . . I've got Friedman on the line, he's going nuts!!!

– Give me the phone, I said, and look after Liza. Take her straight to de Brown.

I took the phone.

– Murchison, is that you, Friedman? What's up, big boy?

– Murchison, you're wrecking my tour. You stir shit wherever you go, don't you?

– Really? I gasped.

– Really; I told you not to follow them, to leave them alone. What do you think you're doing, huh, who said you could go near them, Murchison? Are you listening?

I was busy lighting a cigarette.

– Yeah, yeah, sure, I answered, blowing smoke in his ear.

But he was too far away.

– Well listen to me, you're going to get out now and leave Joe and Maria-Liza be. You've found her, she's alive, everything's fine. Now beat it, I never want to hear your name again.

– Otherwise? I ventured.

– Otherwise! Otherwise! Otherwise!

He was on the verge of choking.

– Otherwise I'll take legal action. Have no doubt I can take legal action. You don't have any right to . . . .

I hung up. I can't stand hysterics on the phone. He could take all the legal action he wanted, I really couldn't give a damn. I dropped by de Brown's dressing room to check things out. The two of them were there, lovingly entwined. I left them undisturbed for a few moments while I wandered down the corridors having a good look around. It was all happening. I watched the auditorium filling up and buzzing with conversation, laughter, and occasional shouts. Two technicians were busy putting the finishing touches to the p.a. system on stage. Going by the ones they were wearing, they must have belonged to the Friends of the Funny T-shirt Club. Each had a large slogan printed across his chest. One inquired innocently: 'If God didn't want chicks eating us, why did he make it look like a hot dog?' The other declared: 'If I'd known I was going to live so long, I'd have taken better care of myself.' I detected two typical examples of Southern and New York humour. I laughed out loud, which attracted their attention. The guy working near me asked me to stand clear of the stage, since the concert was about to start. The lights dimmed in the auditorium just as I stood back, and in my path was the entire band in the middle of a warm-up. You'd have thought they were preparing to run the quarter-mile. I stood to one side to let the performers go past and tried to snatch a quick word with de Brown above the buzz of sound in the auditorium.

– I'll see you right after your concert, Joe. It's serious.

He assented nervously. It was the last thing on his mind at that moment, and he swept right past me just after one of the roadies made the usual introduction and the spotlights went on. Someone must have put new batteries in the drummer's back, for he took off at a tempo that tonight was reminiscent of Custer's cavalry charge at Little Bighorn. It really grabbed the audience and they started stomping in a perfect counterpoint. The volume couldn't have been too loud for them; I couldn't imagine any other explanation. At that point I left the stage, the band and the audience and went back to the dressing rooms. This time I was in no rush. I started looking for Maria-Liza, checking each of the dressing rooms and going right around the back of the stage to back where I'd started. She'd disappeared again. I cursed myself pitilessly for having let her out of my sight, and started scouring the auditorium. I soon gave up, you could hardly move an inch in that furnace. Getting edgy, I crossed backstage again, opening every door I came to, closets and all. I was shouting myself hoarse when I thought I noticed a faint commotion in the end dressing room, de Brown's.

It was locked; I forced it open. I was only slightly surprised to stumble on Liza and Turner, who was hurriedly shoving some small oblong packets inside his Filofax. He saw me land in the room and block the smashed door behind me with a chair and turned white. It was the only way out since the dressing room had no window. Maria-Liza remained blank. She sat down at the dressing table and watched me with about as much interest as if I'd been hired to clean up the place, which was precisely what I'd come to do. Turner tried to say something as I went towards him but he had neither the words nor the time. Especially the time. Before he could utter a sound I was on him, landing a left hook à la Sugar Ray. He lost his balance and his Filofax and everything it contained went flying. I grabbed him as he went down, yanked him back up again and angled his face to meet 90 degrees of knee. There was a sickening thud and Turner collapsed winded and with his jaw crimson. Liza still hadn't lifted a finger. You could have paraded a squad of drum majorettes past her and I don't think she would have batted an eyelid. I left her to her un-thoughts and picked up the tour manager's Filofax. There were a dozen packets stuffed inside it. I opened one at random and guesstimated the brownish powder it contained weighed around two grammes. I took them and marched them over to the wash basin. I took the trouble to open them one after the other and emptied them under a stream of cold water. That brought Liza down to earth, and with her eyes wide with horror, she started to blubber, rocking herself back and forth. Outside, the applause was bringing down the house and the band was segueing into a new number about B-52s over Vietnam.

– Don't do that, no, don't do that, she begged me.

It would have taken a division of green berets to stop me from flushing the demon scag back into the sewers it came from. Liza was crying quietly, and the whole thing made a pitiful sight: the creep knocked out cold, the junkie in tailspin and Mr Clean busy at work. I disposed of the whole stash – they shoot horses, don't they? – and turned my attention to Turner. He was still just about conscious, but his eyes were blank and opaque. He reminded me of when I went fishing now and then near Woodstock with Joe and the look on some fishface after an hour of struggling on the riverbank. I found no better way to bring him round than to dowse his pate with a quart of cold Coca-Cola that was sitting there. He stirred fast enough, snorting and coughing and swearing. I nabbed him by the collar and belt, shook him once or twice and threw him into another table stocked with food and drinks. I stood in front of him and kept him in with the dills. He need a little rest. I felt genuine hatred for this gofer, and I could have blown his brains out without blinking an eyelid. But that's not what I was there for, and anyhow I had a few things to ask him. He was still wriggling, in pain apparently, surrounded by a mixture of warm cold cuts, salads, smelly cheeses and fancy French booze. Slowly, he was turning into a still life. He was becoming almost abstract. I brought him back to realism when I propped him against the wall and slapped his face until he pleaded with me to stop.

– Listen to me, Turner, I'm going to ask you some questions and you're going to give me fast answers. Have you got that?

– Uh, uh, he confirmed.

– I want you to tell me why you're giving smack to Maria-Liza.

My question was precise. It called for an answer in kind. I was going to be disappointed.

– Because . . . because she asks me for it. He got the words out with difficulty.

152

I grabbed him by the hair and whacked his head against the wall. That made him scream.

– I'd like to know why you give smack to Maria-Liza, Turner. Don't tell me it's to make yourself some pocket money or I'll break your fingers, I said, pinning down his right hand.

He took me at my word and his mouth opened, in a prelude to total panic. I stuffed his orifice with a little stale baguette, seven slices to be precise, as Maria-Liza turned away nauseated. Turner started choking again, spluttering breadcrumbs right across the room. He was turning redder and redder in the face, but I stood by and didn't lift a finger as he unblocked his kisser. He belched and spluttered, gulping in deep breaths and gasping away. As soon as he'd calmed down, I took his forefinger and twisted it back as far as it would go without breaking.

– You're cra-a-a-azy, he howled, yodelling to perfection.

– Now, you're going to tell me why, aren't you, Turner?

I felt I'd got to the heart of the matter. From the start I'd concentrated on Liza, but she was a red herring. I had the feeling I was onto a huge trafficking ring, with Turner no more than a middle man. And less than middle after the treatment I was doling out to him. Was it because Belmont knew how serious the situation was that he'd said nothing about it, only asking me to bring back his daughter at all cost? In which case his attitude began to make sense. He was probably afraid to say too much at the start and have me refuse to get involved.

I'd fulfilled my contract 50 per cent, and there and then I made up my mind to take the kid back across the Atlantic, and with her safe that way I could do what I liked. The only problem was that she'd soon be craving another hit and the journey home would turn out to be a nightmare. This all went through my head at the speed of light. In the same split second I thought about the help I'd get from Harry, the odds on success, and the additional tight corners I was bound to get into.

– Why, Turner, why?

His finger was about to snap, and he couldn't speak for the pain. He was caught in a vicious circle nobody could get him out of but me. To convince him thoroughly I turned the pressure on all the way. Then came a clear but unassuming crack and a new scream, which was simultaneously drowned out by the sound of hammering on the dressing room door. There were two guys on the other side bawling out some awful threats at me. In Anglais. They knew my name, and they didn't mind yelling it. In florid prose, they promised me a limited future in which I would discover the joys of passive homosexuality, and end up like a stretch of highway, with a gang of hoods driving all over me and abusing my dead mother.

With my Smith & Wesson now in my hand I fired off a couple to shut them up. They drowned out the concert. I'd fired at the top of the door, not to kill, but to stop the goddamned noise. Two large bulletholes had shredded the doorframe, putting a stop to the verbal abuse.

I checked on Maria-Liza who was staring at me deadeyed. I pulled her up with one arm and put her right behind me, telling her not to let go under any circumstances. Then I took hold of Turner, who was hiccuping inconsiderately. He was on the verge of cracking up. I stuck the barrel of my Magnum under his jaw and kicked the chair aside. The door swung open as Turner started yelling.

– Don't shoot, don't shoot, he's stark raving mad. DON'T SHOOT.

Nobody fired.

– Okay, fellows, I spoke up, I want to see everybody up against the wall to the right of the door. Or I'll blow your pal's brains out. You've got three seconds.

I'd picked the right number. I saw three pathetic roadies in a hurry to comply.

– If you're packing any rods I want to see them all on the floor this minute, I added.

I wasn't ideally placed to check whether they'd taken heed or not. Sideways, we must have looked like a little train. Turner squashed in front of me by my left arm and my right Magnum, and Liza hanging on behind like a wagonload of jelly. I broke our little daisy chain, but kept my gun on Turner. Looking at him, I realised he'd gone off the rails. He was standing in a heap with his arms drooping, while Liza looked as if she was getting a bit more together. She didn't move, waiting for further instructions. I motioned to her to stay put for the moment. I kicked the three jerks' legs back as far as possible away from the wall so as to make it difficult for them to move. I picked two guns off the floor and pocketed them automatically. When I spoke to them I tried to sound as if I meant business.

– I'm taking Turner with me. If you move, he gets it. I don't want to see you move even a toe muscle until the show's over.

I took hold of Turner again and pulled him back into the same position as before. He let himself be handled like a big sack of potatoes with legs. I hooked Liza on again and headed backwards for the exit, keeping the

155

three skunks in my line of fire. They gave the impression they were holding the wall, as if a wild drunken horde was on the other side trying to knock it down with a battering ram. But the only hammering was on the bass drum of the Last Chance. In my rush I didn't notice I'd taken the wrong exit, the one leading into the auditorium. It was too late to turn back. I suspected they'd have realised by now that I was gone and they sure wouldn't be planning to spend the night as buttresses. And boy was I right. I hadn't gone five yards, pushing through the crowd dragging my cargo, when the door burst open again, framing a number of back-lit silhouettes. I have to admit that I wasn't exactly keeping a low profile as I went on my way. With every step I took more and more kids noticed my little convoy, in particular the gun I was all too visibly packing. I roared at Liza not to let go. The Last Chance had just started a really subtle blues number that plunged the sound level down from one thousand to nine hundred decibels. I was almost tempted to stop for a moment or two – I've always been a blues man – but decided this wasn't the right time. Instead, I stepped on it, elbowing my way forward twice as hard. There was more and more commotion around us. My assailants had far more freedom of movement and I could see them gaining ground with every second. They were soon less than two yards away, and they weren't empty-handed. I didn't stop to wonder where they'd got their hardware. I saw it and that was enough. I made a quick inspection of what was above my head, and, seeing it was the balcony ceiling, I fired a warning shot into the plaster. The result was pandemonium. The shot loosed a torrent of shocked screams. Some people threw themselves on the floor while others looked

156

wildly around for the gunman. I made the most of the resulting mêlée to pick up speed and increase the distance between me and my pursuers. The band had heard nothing and went on playing. It would take a mortar attack to make them notice anything. Moments later, four of the bouncers appeared out of nowhere. It wasn't their day off. I was able to duck into the crowd just in time and they went by without seeing us. Inevitably, they ran into the second group, and there followed a set-to that quickly became a general brawl. I kept going, without waiting for the final score, and wound up getting us out into the lobby with the swing doors flapping behind us. Turner was still docile, and I jammed my Magnum into his kidneys so as to make us less conspicuous. Liza, on the other hand, was becoming more and more wide awake and alert to my every instruction. I dragged my little retinue as far as the main door, and glanced out into the street. The limousines were still there with their drivers. Turner's presence had become superfluous and I gave him a smart chop on the back of the neck with the butt of my gun. He collapsed on the pavement as if somebody'd stuck a pin in the potato sack. A few passing rubbernecks set up their hue and cry: 'My God', 'Help', and similar hogwash. I took Liza by the hand and towed her towards the car at a run. We jumped inside and I told the guy to get the lead out. He wasn't fazed, and we were treated to a Cape Kennedy lift-off. I turned round to see what was happening outside the Casino. I saw about ten characters rushing into the roadway. One of them pointed feverishly at the limo. At once the pointer and the rest bundled into two other cars parked a few yards back. We were in for one helluva chase.

157

SIXTEEN

I've no idea why but I suddenly remembered I'd completely forgotten to phone Belinda. She'd be getting worried sick, imagining the worst. In the heat of the moment the most humdrum things can take on a strange importance. When I noticed a telephone right in front of me I realised why I'd thought of it. The limo had shot headlong down the street that led to Place Clichy, and I looked back in the direction of the Casino. I could make out headlights zigzagging down the street, to the vehement accompaniment of car horns. I made a polite suggestion to the coachman that he step on the gas. He'd caught on there was something unusual happening, and I wasted no time enlightening him.

– Listen, buddy, I know it's not part of your job description, but we've got some ugly customers following us and what they've got in mind could be terminal! If you stick with us I'll make it worth your while, I said, pulling two nice 500 franc bills out of my pocket.

He stared at the notes in the rearview, then at my earnest expression, and finally at the cars on our heels.

– Okay, it's a deal, he said, reaching out for the dough with his left hand. That would keep him well-oiled.

– We'll shake them, don't worry.

He put his foot down and the Mercedes went into hyperdrive. Luckily the lights at the end of the road were green and we crossed the square burning rubber like a hotrod. We came out onto another avenue with a bit more traffic and inaugurated a third lane off to the left, which cut one out for the oncoming cars. This all made for a nice mess and a heap of scraped paintwork. Maria-Liza hung on in her corner without a murmur. Either she had guts or she was out of her head, which comes down to the same thing. I took a quick check on the tail party. I couldn't see the cars any more, though this didn't make our driver lose any speed. He had everything under control and was manoeuvring with unmistakable expertise. I took advantage of this little lull to lift the phone and dial Belinda's number, forgetting it was 5 in the morning in New York. Her sleepy voice answered after two or three rings.

– Sam, at last! I was so worried, she blurted.

– You shouldn't be, Belinda sweetie, I assured her, it's practically like being on vacation here.

That was no excuse for staying on the line another couple of hours, especially since I'd checked again and noticed that at least one of the two cars was back on course.

– Belinda, I'm sort of busy right now. I just wanted to give you the privilege of hearing my voice. Don't worry, everything's fine, and I'll call you again tomorrow for longer. Bye.

– But Sam . . . .

I hung up.

159

– What's your name, I asked the driver.

– Louis.

– Okay, Louis, they're still on our tail, can you get us out of this?

– We're coming up to the ring road, he explained. I think the smartest thing would be to lose them in the suburbs. I know a good place. Do you trust me?

– With my eyes closed!

– Then let's go!

He slammed the horn, flashing his headlights. That cleared a path. All the same we nearly ran smack into an unsuspecting bus that Louis managed to avoid just in time by running onto the sidewalk which, miraculously, happened to be clear just there, except for two huge garbage cans that soon found new inspiration as meteorites. But the other guys were closing in, and the second car was now nose to tail with the first. When we got to a small square at the bottom of the avenue, Louis went for broke. Jamming on the brakes and screeching into reverse, he did a splendid half turn, swerved to an angle almost facing back the way we'd come and placed the limousine just out of sight from the main road. When they got there they wouldn't see us until the last possible moment, while we would have the luxury of at least three whole seconds to anticipate their reaction. No sooner had we spotted the hood ornament of the first car than he took off like a bat out of hell and bombed right between the two cars, which were maybe five yards apart. It was totally suicidal, but we've all got to die one day.

– Hang on to your hats, he yelled.

I flung myself on top of Liza to cover her. I mean, to protect her. We passed within an inch behind the first car, which, seeing us without warning, swerved to the right in a move that was equally fatal for a disposal

160

truck parked by the pavement. The second car escaped our flanking attack by a hair's breadth, and I heard the radiator grille scratching the length of our right side with a noise like a beehive gone mad. The driver was so terrified by the recklessness of our manoeuvre that he completely lost control, letting his dandy roadster career off in the direction of a metro entrance. Poor slob – he sure would need a new car.

I let go of Liza to give Louis a round of applause. I'd turned up an ace driver. He had cool, he had nerve and the air conditioning had nothing to do with it. For a moment he took his foot lightly off the accelerator; two traffic cops had just turned up to take over.

– *Merde*, he griped, we could have done without this.

I took out two crisp bills and handed them to him.

– Another ride round the block, Louis.

He pocketed them with a smile and a retort:

– Done, boss.

And it was, for after taking two right turns, he drove us into a factory yard between two trucks, killing the engine and all the lights. This guy knew the town like the well-greased palm of his hand. The cops went past right under our noses without noticing, and we parked there for a while, taking five before diving back into the traffic. I used the time to give some thought to the situation, which seemed kind of sticky. Here I was in a city I didn't know, I didn't know a word of the local lingo, but I had a genius of a driver who didn't think twice about sticking his neck out for us and, less excitingly, a paralytic girl who was tagging along without a word. There was no way she could go back there. I wasn't very clear about what I was going to do with her, but whatever it was, she wouldn't end up back in the clutches of those sharks.

161

Daddy Belmont had neglected to put me in the picture, and I'd find my own way of thanking him when I got back. I'd got it into my head to save this poor kid's skin, and it would have taken a dozen avalanches to make me change my mind. What I couldn't come up with, though, was some place where we could hole up and breathe easy. The hotel was sunk, the Casino likewise. I mentioned it to Louis. He didn't take long to give me an answer.

– I've a suggestion to make. I'm friendly with a bikers' club in the inner suburbs and I can ask them to put you up for a few days if you like. In exchange for some cash, naturally.

I could have turned down this offer, but it looked good enough to me. Who'd ever dream of looking for us in a place like that? Liza had no thoughts on the matter; she just lit a cigarette. I did the same and offered one to Louis.

– It's a deal, pal. Can you guarantee we'd be safe there?

– Safe as can be, he pronounced. But don't expect a four-star hotel, you'll be disappointed.

I got the picture. But comfort has never been my first priority. I've always preferred security, even though some people claim the two are inseparable. I was starting to feel a little peckish and I asked Louis to make a stop on the way at some quiet restaurant. He took us to the Porte de la Villette neighbourhood at a comparative crawl. I turned my attention to Liza who was still slumped like a zombie in her corner. Fat tears rolled down her cheeks. I patted her hand to comfort her, the way I'd seen it done in a documentary about apes. She gave me a little lost smile then threw herself desperately into my arms. She was in a state of virtual collapse. I breathed in the sweet perfume that rose

162

from her hair and held her close, like a woodcutter getting ready to uproot a birch tree.

– Everything's going to be fine now, relax.

For the first time in what seemed ages she spoke up.

– I don't understand what's happening, Mr Murchison. Who are all these people? What have they all got against Joe and me?

– I don't know whether they've got something against you and him, or just against you, I ventured, but I'd venture there'll be more surprises in store. You can trust me.

I couldn't really make out why Turner's pals were so hellbent. I'd hardly scratched him and it had unleashed a pitched battle. I was sure all this was connected with the earlier attempts to rub me out, but there was a missing link.

Louis thoughtfully parked the car out of the way behind a delivery van. It was a bona fide Parisian eatery, he told me, unable to resist commenting on the place. If discretion was a Parisian trait then this dive got full marks. Besides a few drunks propping up the bar and two other tables occupied by drooling couples, the place was deserted. Louis told me that at the weekend though, there was barely room to move. Accordionists livened up the evenings and got the customers shuffling round the floor. Missing out on that had been a blessing.

I chose a table at the far end and settled Liza and Louis opposite me. With my back to the wall I kept one eye on the door, just in case. I ordered three ribs of beef, salads and beer, but Louis insisted on having some vino. I seconded the motion, listening distractedly as he boosted the joint's culinary merits. I cut in fast to steer him towards the subject of his bikers and whatever he could tell me about them. He'd known

163

them for about ten years, before 'settling down' – it was probably why he'd gone in for driving – he'd knocked around on the same circuit himself. From what I could tell they were equivalent to those American drop outs who spend most of their time in the saddle or drinking, or both, asking for only one thing: to be left in peace. Should circumstances prove otherwise, they were well able to defend themselves, and it was best to give them a wide berth. They lived well away from civilisation, in a big place full of Harleys, and, according to Louis, they would ask no questions, on condition we kept our noses out of their business. All this sounded fine by me. I told him so and he went and made a quick phone call to tell them we were on our way. This time I had no trouble in having them re-cook my meat which, naturally, was drowning in blood. I wondered why they bothered killing the livestock in this country. It was actually well done on the rebound and I had to admit that it was damn good, nearly as good as at Peter Lueger's in Brooklyn. Liza scarcely touched her food and I had to wheedle, like with a faddy kid, to get her to swallow a few mouth-fuls. Louis asked shyly if he could finish what was on her plate, and Liza jumped at the opportunity to get rid of it. But it had put some colour back in her cheeks. She still looked just as vague, maybe more like resigned. I was fairly certain she wouldn't try to run away. She felt she could trust me, and that I was the only thing that made sense in the whole mess. She was worried, though, about what Joe would think, especially when he got Turner's version of what happened. I reassured her as best I could and promised that at the first opportunity I'd let her get in touch with de Brown. Even that didn't seem to cheer her up much. It was like nothing was really getting through

164

to her. She wanted the whole nightmare to be over and to be left in peace with her boyfriend. I guaranteed the former and avoided the latter. When we'd finished eating I asked for the bill and some coffee, and got the tab. I didn't want to spend forever in that joint. There was no way of being sure our limo hadn't been reported to the cops and that there weren't patrol cars out on our trail at that very moment. I felt a lot better, and I saw life in a more favourable light. I signed to Louis, who thanked me for the dinner, then the three of us got up and left the restaurant.

They would have had trouble renting out the neighbourhood for a remake of Mary Poppins. Dim street lamps threw a faint light on the sidewalk and the cobblestones, which were swept at intervals by the yellowish flares of passing cars. The shadow of a disused factory towered from across the road, like a ruined castle.

– All we need now is rain, I muttered, just as the first drops of a new downpour began to fall on us.

Louis crossed the suburb at cruising speed, maintaining it was bristling with unseen cops on the lookout. He was probably right, because the streets were emptier than the première of *Heaven's Gate*. I lit a cigarette and watched the houses go by, block after block. The scenery was dark and dismal, lifeless. No neon signs, all the shops locked up with iron shutters, a solitary passer-by letting Fido take a leak; we could have been in any American small town, with just a touch more claustrophobia. Our car sailed along at the leisurely pace of a night steamer, with the radio oozing Jimmy Reed, to inject a note of gaiety. I was amazed they were playing such good stuff and told Louis.

– It's not the radio, he put me straight, all you hear on it is shit. I do my own cassettes, it's more reliable.

Yeah, I sure liked this guy. We talked a bit, enough for him to tell me about his past, when he was something of a hellraiser. He'd made a few blunders when he was younger, in the days when he was up against the whole world. He'd paid for it and, though he didn't disown it, he was happier with a quiet life making ends meet without making any waves. Anyway, he enjoyed ferrying the fat cats, it made him feel like a baa-lamb. From emirs to crooners he'd seen quite an array of specimens warm the back seat. He assured me it was a way of life that meant he never needed to go to the movies. But you're the wildest I've had since I started, he added flatteringly.

I thanked him.

Our jaunt was nearly over; he stopped in front of a huge gateway, sounding his horn. A couple of minutes later somebody let us in, and Louis drove the car into an open lot that could have passed for a scrapyard. The remains of old tyres were heaped up together in the middle of piles of sheet metal, bike frames and other unidentifiable objects, though not flying ones. I hoped so anyway. A bearded grease-encrusted giant of a guy came up to Louis's car door and waited for introductions. Louis didn't even know my name.

– Sam Murchison, I cut in, ready to shake hands, and Maria-Liza. Delighted.

– Jeff, the mountain ranged, turning.

He waved us on to follow him inside a ruin whose dilapidated state would have killed the architect who'd designed it probably a couple of thousand years ago. The roof was gone, so it seemed, and the occupants had covered the gaping hole as best they could with plastic. There must have been a clear view of the sky from the first floor.

– Why settle for four stars, when you can have them all? I asked Louis.

SEVENTEEN

Big Jeff spoke English about as well as I speak Hungarian, in other words not well, and Louis soon proved indispensable for communication with the other tenants. I counted a dozen of them scattered over a sizeable area whose tasteful décor consisted entirely of a big bar, a big TV, a big billiard table and a few armchairs. An inside staircase led to the floor above, while a door down at the end showed the way to the cellar. A few posters wilted on the walls; mostly they were of choppers, or portraits of Sioux and Cherokee warriors, but there were a few stroke book spreads too. The whole thing was dowsed in reasonably okay country music. Our arrival didn't create much of a stir, and most of these erstwhile cowboys even made a point of ignoring us and turned their backs, which gave me plenty of opportunity to decipher their colours. From what you could make out their club must have been called The Rattlesnakes. Done in a gothic semicircle, the name over-arched a stylised snake's head. Lower down, as a finishing touch, came the letters M.C. followed by Paris.

If they weren't our old Hell's Angels, they were doing all they could to look like them. But I hadn't

come to do a sociological study of nomadic sub-
cultures. Jeff introduced five or six club members and
invited us to follow him to an area of the room where
we sat round a table that was set up for a poker game.
Louis detailed the situation with a succinctness any
rabbi would have envied. I padded a bit to make it
clear to his pal that things were even more serious and
that the story wasn't over. I was expecting trouble any
moment. He didn't seem impressed. He got Louis to
translate that his club gave us its protection out of
friendship for Louis, and that he'd already heard more
than enough. He didn't give a flying fuck about my
stories. We were to make ourselves at home, and so
long as we were here we'd have nothing to be afraid
of. I liked his attitude and I thanked him warmly. I told
Louis I wanted to pay them for their trouble, but he
rejected the idea, claiming it would be taken as an
insult. He pointed at the bar, to a box that was used as
the band's kitty, and for any fines that came up. There
and then I got up and took out a wad of ten 500 franc
bills, then went over and put them in their money box
without saying a word. There was no reaction from
any of them, except Jeff, who nodded in acknowledge-
ment when I went back to the table. I liked this
system, and I felt immediately that it worked. I
sneaked another quick look at Maria-Liza, who was
coming down hard from her high and was staring at
the deck of cards, quietly shaking. Without a word to
me, Louis made a request to Jeff and he shouted for
somebody called Clara. Clara appeared from the other
end of the room along with another girl. Like their
men they were tattooed and poured into skintight
jeans that looked like they were laundered in engine
oil. Clara's English was more civilised, and she tried to
make contact with Liza once Jeff had explained one or

two things. I tried to persuade the Belmont kid to go with the two chicks and after a few minutes she took some notice. She wasn't looking too good, and I watched her go off, supported either side by Clara and Co. as if she was going to shatter into a thousand pieces any moment. The three of them disappeared into the other room and I returned to my immediate problem. First of all I wanted to reach Harry, to see if he could do anything.

Louis brought me a phone and I tried the hotel. But Harry hadn't come back and he hadn't left any message. I cursed the whole kit 'n' caboodle: the hotel, Harry, his room and his floosie. He would have come in really handy right then. I tried putting a different complexion on the future, but the horizon was so overcast it looked like a full-blown storm was brewing. I've never been hot on meteorology, but even a dead frog would have concurred. Jeff offered us a drink and we went over to the bar to hoist one. He announced my name to nobody in particular, and nobody in particular answered with a smattering of indifferent greetings. I doubt whether a goods train passing straight through the club would have attracted their attention. Fortuitously, there was no railroad station in the neighbourhood.

As we were drinking our beer, Jeff asked us to go round the other side of the bar. He pulled us behind a curtain that hung across a recess in the wall.

– Our collection, he said with a certain pride, pointing to three racks packed to overflowing with weapons of every calibre.

They were some collectors. From the Winchester 1873 or 94 to Mossberg pump-action shotguns, by way of Remington Rolling Blocks, it could lay claim to being a gun nut's paradise. I gave a whistle of admiration as I took in both the quantity and the quality. The one doesn't necessarily rule out the other.

– Are they expecting the Red Army, or what? I asked Louis.

– No, no, he said, breaking up, it's an absolutely genuine collection. Legally, they can't take a single thing out of the building, and all they usually do is take them apart and put them back together again.

I relished the 'usually'. I showed off my own 357; Jeff felt bound to show it some respect. But I knew very well it was only a popgun in comparison with their strike force. I took this opportunity to reload it. On the other hand, my 'Quick Defence' bullets aroused genuine interest. I boasted about their penetration power and reliability. I gave three to Jeff. It was the most I could manage since I was only carrying three spare clips. But he showed a connoisseur's appreciation. They themselves were hardly short of ammo, for I could count several thousand rounds of Parabellums, Mauser 7.64s, Winchester 243s, Magnum 44s, not to mention diverse other shotgun shells and slugs.

We stayed there for a while, absorbed in gun buffs' talk. Gradually, I could feel Jeff warming to me, and within half an hour we were taking turns at slapping one another on the back. It made us thirsty. We were kidding over another round of drinks when an idea occurred to me. Blackwell and his 747s. Anxiously I searched for his number and found it by some miracle deep in my pocket. He was there, and what's more I woke him up.

– Who's the son-of-a-bitch that . . . ?

– Cool it, Jimmy. It's me, Sam, Sam Murchison.

– Dumb ass, it's no time of night to be calling up working guys, he snapped, it's 1.30!

171

– The world belongs to night owls.

– You writing poetry or what?

– Jimmy, listen, it's serious. I've got some big problems and maybe you can give me a hand.

He almost calmed down.

– Oh! Oh! Oh!!! Sam Murchison's got problems. Going in for tautologies these days?

Jimmy had always been one for fancy words. I went straight to the point.

– Can an American with her passport in order get back into the States even if she doesn't want to go?

He made me repeat the question three times before he risked getting my meaning.

– You kidding or what?

– Do I sound like it?

He admitted I didn't.

– It's virtually impossible. I mean you can always get somebody through with their passport in order if you give them massive doses of tranquillisers (perfect for Liza). But afterwards, there's nothing to guarantee that the person won't sue. And that can go very wrong. For the pilot and especially for the company. You can imagine.

He was quite right.

– Forget about flying, he went on, and try a sea route. And take care of this repatriation yourself. Don't try and involve anybody else, it's too risky.

I bowed to his superior wisdom and thanked him for his advice.

– Listen, old buddy, it would have been a pleasure, but I'm sure you understand. How serious is it?

– Any more serious and I'd be dying of boredom, I said reassuringly.

– Is there anything else I can do, Sam?

172

– No, leave it. See you one of these days, Jimmy, and keep an eye on your liver.

– I'd do better getting a nurse for that, he wise-cracked. But I could feel he wasn't in the mood for laughs. I hung up, pissed off. Very pissed off. The moment I left this hideyhole with Maria-Liza under my arm, I'd have to get across the frontier as fast as possible. Where, when and how was still vague as ever. And what about who I'd find waiting for me if I put so much as a foot out the door. I lit a cigarette and I thought about all this, then I had a word with Louis. He took the view that the wisest thing was to stay put for a few days. The band left Paris the following day and usually everyone went with them. In the circumstances he could say I'd taken him hostage or that he'd made a choice to stay with me. For now the best thing was to lie low.

It was then that we heard shouting from the next room. We all turned towards the open door, exchanging puzzled looks. It was Maria-Liza castigating her two guardian angels. I rushed towards them, erupting into a room full of bike skeletons with a mattress on the floor. Liza sat curled up on it. She was vituperating, as they say in the kind of books you can't buy at a newspaper kiosks. She was looking her old self – the one that would have inspired any of George Romero's casting directors – and she was venting her spleen on the two unfortunates and they weren't taking it very well.

– She's really flipped, one said.
– She's cracking up, the other said.

And there was a third who said nothing, because she wasn't there.

It wasn't a pretty sight. Little Liza's teeth were chattering and her skin looked like cold turkey. Her nose was running and she had dilated pupils like a hungry cat's eyes. She was bitching about a terrible pain in her stomach and asking in a little voice – or screaming – for a fix. Quick, RIGHT NOW. I realised maybe I should have kept some for her, if I'd wanted to avoid this home detox cure. The two girls were looking at me as if they expected to see me produce a syringe. I wasn't too happy about that. I made it abundantly clear they were mistaken.

– We're up shit creek, said Clara. She should take downers, otherwise there'll be three days of this.

I couldn't see myself putting up with this nightmare for as long as that without it shredding my nerves.

– The best thing, said Louis, would be anti-hypertensives, but they're on prescription, and I don't think calling a doctor here would go down very well.

– We could always give her a hot bath, Clara suggested, but I'd have to take her to my place.

I thought I'd noticed there was no bathtub in the place. What the hell would be the point in a bikers' club anyway?

Maria-Liza was going from worse to worst and the girls had to hold her down to stop her from throwing herself at the wall. Jeff didn't look entirely delighted with the turn of events. I was going to ask Louis to put him in the picture when one of the bikers who was acting as lookout on the first floor – I hadn't even noticed him till then – stuck his head out at the top of the stairs to tell us that a car had just driven slowly past the building for the third time. It wasn't a cop car, he knew them all inside out. The news set off a ripple of excitement. Jeff went up to get a closer look, while everyone downstairs went over to the boarded-up windows to peer through the slits. In less than five minutes there was another shout from the lookout:

174

– There they are again, look, there they are again.

It was his final shout. A split second later a bullet hit his forehead. His arms whirled wildly before he plunged backwards onto the stairs.

He fell violently to the floor fifteen feet below, followed by Jeff who had tried his best to break his fall.

It was chaos on the ground floor. It was like someone had let a rat loose at a feminist meeting. People were yelling and running in every direction.

Two of the greasers grabbed weapons quicker than it takes a Japanese to spell Mitsubishi, and rushed for the stairs. A barrage of fire stopped them in their tracks. In the thick of the mêlée I ran to the alcove to get a pump-action shotgun and ammo, then I came back to the main room and, difficult as it was, got everyone to be quiet. Hearing footsteps, I looked up and saw two men at the top of the stairs, hesitating on their way down. I checked the shotgun was loaded and took rough aim at the ceiling. The first shot was right on target and was followed by a horrified scream. A body fell on the floor above us, and we could tell from the sound of footsteps that somebody else was trying to make a run for it. An assault party of five or six club members took the stairs and disappeared up them shooting in every direction. Jeff was examining his buddy, but he realised there was nothing more to be done. His face was a mixture of boiling rage and incredulity. He stared at me, red with fury.

– Jesus Christ, what's going on, what the hell *is* this?

I didn't have the time to go into it, but it was evident the other guys were on to us. I took the stairs four at a time. Upstairs I found my victim twitching on the floor as if somebody had torn off his privates. And they had, for that matter. He was surrounded by the earlier arrivals, who weren't exactly trying to alleviate his suffering. They were working him over, kicking him in the ribs and the head, and spitting on the bastard, who couldn't have felt much by now given the nature of his wound. His whole groin was shot away and most of his guts were on the floor. I was about to ask them to cool it when an extra hard kick broke his neck, clean. They went on kicking what was left of him for a while, venting their fury. They were all making such a racket that I almost didn't hear the screeching of tyres in the street. I ventured a cautious look, just in time to see three cars packed to overflowing with armed capos, skidding to a halt at the corner of the street and in front of the gate. Without stopping to think I levelled the riot-gun and shot my second shell at the nearest car. When he'd stopped the driver had skidded into reverse, which mean I had him in profile. I had taken aim without thinking, and the result was more than I could have hoped for. A tremendous explosion rocked the street, suddenly setting the dim street lamps ablaze and shattering all the glass within a radius of over forty feet. The blaze gave me a clear view of about a dozen guys flushed out by the wave of heat and buzzing off like mosquitoes facing a jet of RAID. None of them had so much as a scratch. They must have lit some candles before coming to see us. As for the guy who'd made off from our direction, he was busy landing between two of the cars.

I raised the alarm and took charge of operations. I placed three gunmen at the broken-down windows, using sign language to stress the need for caution. I didn't have time to hear myself elaborate, for there was a terrific salvo that shook the reinforced door giving onto the street. The hoodlums weren't stinting themselves. They were doing a regular Pearl Harbor. I went back down the stairs, taking them five at a time now.

– All we need now is for them to hit us with grenades, I thought, just as a whopper of an explosion rocked the whole of the first floor.

THEY DID HAVE GRENADES!!!

All hell was let loose downstairs. The building was being machine-gunned from outside with nobody able to return the fire. Upstairs, meanwhile, there wasn't a sound to be heard. Everybody had dug in, weapons at the ready. I found myself beside Louis; he was biting his nails.

– It's me, he whimpered, the whole thing's my fault. Oh no! I don't believe it!

– Relax, man, I said, trying to calm him down, it's not your fault, nobody followed us.

– Yes they did, it's my fault, I completely forgot about the transmitter in the limousine. We got here so fast I didn't think to disconnect it. It means HQ knew where we were all along. The other guys only had to ask them.

I didn't congratulate him, and anyway I had more important things to do. Then again I've never gone overboard for wailing walls. Even if I had been that way, what happened next would have hipped me to the advantages of action. The door leading to the yard, for all its reinforcement, gave way to a second grenade that blew it off easily and sent it airborne.

Fortunately, the club's residents were no novices, and they immediately answered with a torrent of gunfire that made sure nobody could get near the entrance. There were even three of them doing a kamikaze routine, creeping along the walls to get closer to the gap. They managed to position themselves either side of it, spraying anything that moved in the yard. I applauded their initiative that prevented any more grenades getting inside the house. I think the third one might have been unlucky. Everybody was taking cover, and I'd taken up a good position. But in almost total darkness I could only fire haphazardly. The guy nearest the opening signalled to his partner, and in a single move the two of them sprang outside, to be replaced at once by two reinforcements. These guys knew how to handle themselves, just as if stuff like this happened to them every day. It made me think the roof must have been lifted off in some aerial bombardment, and that at weekends they turned into a training base. I couldn't see any other explanation. Anyway, these kids had plenty of guts. There was machine-gun fire going off in all directions, and one of the two intrepid warriors suddenly reappeared, driven back by a charge of buckshot that had just torn his chest apart. The situation was insane, but I couldn't see a way out of it.

While the street door held I made up my mind to forestall a frontal attack, and recruited four volunteers that I positioned alongside it. I loosened and shot back the heavy bolt. In one quick move I opened it wide while four rifles began to sweep the area outside. We hit several targets, at random. Most of the vehicles parked at the front of the club were now scrapyard fodder. Still, it was industry's gain. I saw three bodies lying in the middle of the road and added a fourth to make an even number. Ninety per cent of the widows in the street had their lights on, but nobody was taking the risk of opening them, especially since a lot of them were being blown to smithereens one after the other, producing fresh screams to enhance the general carnage. I was so busy clearing the street that I com-

178

pletely forgot about Maria-Liza. It was my only mistake. I saw her crossing the room, a distraught and deathly pale figure at the centre of the storm. She threw her arms as if to tear her hair out. I remained powerless as she headed straight for what was left of the door to the yard. She had no time to poke her nose outside. A big motherfucker of a bullet tore off half her head and she was thrown six feet backwards, her body squirming in convulsions. She'd gotten her fix.

I scrambled towards her to check the damage, and had to fight to keep my food down. She was a certifiable write-off and nobody could do anything more for her. With fire in my belly I went back to my post, and to shooting up the street. I wanted to finish off every single one of these bastards. People were falling all around me like flies, and the situation was getting hopeless, when the question that must have been on the lips of fifteen thousand neighbours: 'Where are the forces of law and order?' finally got an answer. They had arrived, sirens blaring.

EIGHTEEN

Oddly, for a few moments nothing much changed, and the mutual extermination went on, with everyone showing as much interest in the arrival of the cops as in the first test-tube baby. Then, just as suddenly, as if by magic our adversaries disappeared. When I turned round I made a rapid inventory. There were eight of us still standing. Daniel and Jeff were lying in pools of their own blood, one across the bar and the other beside him, a goner. There were people dying all around us in among the fallen plaster, broken furniture and exploded bottles of beer. Clara and her friend were hunched over some of the wounded, totally horrified. The sirens were getting closer and closer, and the survivors ditched their Red Crosses for the sake of a fast getaway. I had some scruples about doing the same, but at the same time I'd have been no good to anybody if I'd stayed in the vicinity. I crossed the back yard, which was no longer just a car cemetery – as the poet says, there's no cemetery so lovely as to make us want to stay – and started scaling the back wall, giving myself a boost on the carcass of a despatch rider. I assumed the whole neighbourhood would be thoroughly cop-ridden.

And I was extra careful when I found myself in a tiny alleyway parallel to the street. You could hear whistles blowing all over the place, only drowned out by the cops' sirens. I slipped under a doorway arch and did a reccie before taking another step. The alley ran between a row of warehouses whose outlines I could only guess at through the darkness. There was only one way out and it happened to be in the direction that was crawling with fuzz. I started out by heading for the other end and found myself facing a thirty-foot wall. My mountaineering boots had been left in my studio back in New York and modesty prevented me from attempting the climb barehanded. When I took a look at the frontage of the last shed I saw a gleam of hope. A metal girder about seven or eight feet above the ground stuck out into the middle of the alley as a hoist support. I took a flying leap towards it with an enthusiasm fuelled by despair. By some miracle I managed to catch hold of it the first time. I heaved myself up with difficulty and did a balancing act on top of it to reach the wall. At the end of it was an oval window that was recessed by a tiny fraction of an inch. I was just about to touch it when I saw a car driving into the alley and bouncing boys-in-blue light off the walls. In a split second I was huddled in the corner, not moving so much as a muscle. So long as they didn't take it into their heads to come further down the alley, I'd be safe. I said a prayer to St Valentine and he had the kindness to lend an ear to my plight. The cop car stopped beside the wall I'd crossed less than ten minutes earlier. Four officers got out, guns at the ready, and took cover behind their vehicle. I couldn't hear any more shots being fired. The party was over, at least for everyone else. I groped behind my back and realised I was leaning against a windowpane nobody had thought of cleaning for at least a century. I decided it was time to have it replaced. I took off my jacket, wrapped it tight around my Magnum, and, under cover of the racket outside, I thudded against it. There was a muffled shattering of glass and I thrust my hand in up to the wrist to open the frame. All this happened in silence, or at least more quietly than what was coming from the house and around it. At any rate the gendarmes in the dead end hadn't noticed anything, they were so busy anticipating what might loom up and hit them, and on listening to every word that sparked out of their walkie-talkies. I slipped into a lumber room of some kind, as warily as a grunt in a minefield. Inside, I gave myself a few seconds to get my breath back and take my bearings. I could hardly believe that the little going-over I'd given Turner had unleashed such mayhem. Or was he just a very sensitive guy? No, what was at stake in this whole business was something inestimably more valuable, namely little Maria-Liza. So I'd have been interested to see their faces when they discovered she'd left this vale of tears for evermore. But what did they want from her and why had they gone to such incredible lengths to try and get her back? As far as I was concerned the mystery remained. Her father sent me to look for her, I found her drugged to the eyeballs and as soon as I'd touched a hair on her head I had a whole army after my ass. There was enough there to run a mystery serial in the *New York Times* puzzles section for a good year. I swore somehow I'd get an answer in the next twenty-four hours. I felt the strain of nervous exhaustion and had a yen to wind down and sleep for a few hours. As is the case with millions of my kind, sleep is the best way I've ever found of clearing my head. But I considered

182

this to be an inadvisable yen, and, tireless worker as I am, I decided to go on ploughing the furrow of my destiny. It was time for some germination, and it had to be real soon. Still, I took time out to light a cigarette, without going so far as to send smoke signals through the window. Minutes later, I was groping my way out of my box, once I'd spotted a dwarf-sized door opposite. It was tricky to open, but it was worth it. What I found, steeped in a grey half-light, was a vast shed full of wooden boxes. The silence that enveloped it was soothing for sick nerves, and mine qualified. Letting my eyes get used to the darkness, I went to find an emergency exit. A ladder propped against one of the walls reached just under the roof and ended an inch or so away from a small window. I shot up it and got to the top in record time. I made a mental note to officially check this later and took the lie of the land up here where the air was purer. I saw what looked like a security system, in other words an electronic alarm, which got me cursing under my breath. I was nearly forty feet up, and I reckoned, with unimpeachable logic, it was bound to be the same on the other side. The question now was: should I stay stuck there like a ham dangling from a hook, and risk the gendarmes seeing me when they roll in for a routine search, or else go for broke and face the void. I was getting pins and needles in my legs and I preferred the devil that I didn't know. I gripped the lever like mad and with an abrupt movement pushed the whole thing out. It was indeed an alarm. The warehouse was filled with frenzied vibrations, as if six foghorns had formed a choir. I propelled myself through the window opening with another prayer to old Valentine, and just managed to keep my footing. I'd have been a hit in any circus with a trick like that. Then, clutching onto whatever I could

183

get a hold of, I eased myself round as carefully as possible, and took the precaution of closing the window again. It would take them a little while to locate the break-in. Once I'd gotten my footing back, I took my bearings, unimpressed by the din below. My eyes had got quite used to the darkness and I could almost see clearly now. It was looking good. The rooftops were all edge to edge and there was no need for me to climb back down on this side. I advanced one step at a time, in no rush, and in ten minutes I'd got halfway to the end of the cul de sac. When I looked back I saw that my warehouse had visitors. I pictured them checking all the wooden boxes to flush out the intruder. I wished them good luck and continued on my perilous way. I ended up above the drop onto the main street; I stretched myself flat to take a look. It was like 6 p.m. on Broadway. I counted something like ten squad cars, six ambulances, eight traffic cops and a fire engine extension ladder. Not to mention the crowd on the sidewalk and at the apartment windows. By comparison, an anthill on speed would have looked like Salt Lake City on a Sunday Mormon, uh, morning. Of course everybody was much more concerned with what was happening down there than on the roof tops. All the same I metamorphosed into Spiderman to shimmy down the drainpipes where the corner would keep me out of sight. It's one of the most dangerous sports I know, especially when you weigh going on for two hundred pounds. But I have fun doing it. In less than no time I was six feet off the ground, and gave it all a once-over before I cast myself.

I mingled discreetly with the herd, then went off in the opposite direction to the police roadblock I'd seen before. They were all parlez-ing away in that funny language, but I didn't ask for a running translation. As

I walked I shook off some of the eighty-eight pounds of dust I'd accumulated along the way. I straightened my tie and lit a well-deserved cigarette. I walked for a hundred yards and came to a crossroads thick with signs. I saw a sign for Paris on the left and opted for the capital. The countryside's never been my thing. It would have been dangerous to take the main road, but there was such a commotion there that it made me feel safer than I'd feel in an empty street. I quickened my pace some and soon put a respectable distance between me and the scene of the crime. Two crossroads further on I made up my mind to get away from the main road and to keep going in the same direction by way of side streets. I looked at my watch: it was 2.45. It took me at least an hour and a half to reach the outskirts of Paris. Once I was there I thought I could risk a taxi but finding one turned out to be a little harder than finding a gleam of compassion in the eyes of Russkie Politbureau member. On the verge of appropriating the first thing I saw on four wheels, I finally succeeded. Yet again I'd come within a hair's breadth of crime and I wiped my brow with profound relief.

The one I came up with this time wasn't into transcendental meditation. He had his radio on at something like four hundred watts, and I sat right in the middle to make the most of the stereo separation. At least it ruled out conversation.

– Are you English? he yelled.

I pretended to be falling asleep and he didn't persist. It was something of an achievement, with all the noise that was washing over me. Loud voices bawled out of the radio in between jingles that would have emptied Bloomingdale's in three minutes flat. I couldn't understand a single word of this barrage, any more than I could make out the music.

I put up with this torture stoically all the way to the hotel, where caution prompted me to have him drop me at the street corner. I walked past the Warwick twice to see how the land lay, but everything seemed as quiet as ever. Maybe I'd gone deaf. As I lit a fresh Winston, my lighter's familiar click reassured me. I went into the lobby and woke a dozing night porter. He handed me my key along with a wad of messages that I pocketed on my way to the elevators. I decided to walk up the two flights, and moved noiselessly with my 357 at the ready. The older I get the more suspicious I get. There was dead silence as I checked to see if the piece of cellophane was still sticking out. It wasn't there. I stood listening at my door for five minutes until I was almost certain there was nobody inside. I turned the key, quieter than a mouse, and instinctively assumed an offensive stance, holding out both arms ready to shoot. Nobody in sight. I slammed the door shut with a kick then carried out a thorough search of the suite, checking behind the curtains and making sure the windows were closed. I got undressed and permitted myself a cold, but not ice-cold, shower. I towelled myself dry and at the same time poured myself a double Jack Daniels on the rocks, and knocked it back in one. I felt a lot better and ready to take on some new problems. I put on a fresh change of clothes, an immaculate suit, and heaped all my things in my travelling bag. My watch showed it was 4.55. When I looked at the messages I saw an awful lot of people had tried to reach me that evening. Belinda, Belmont, Cardier, and Harry, who left me the address of the restaurant he was in a few hours ago. I'd made up my mind not to hang around, since things

186

were likely to get pretty hot for me in the not too distant future, and I had to find a way to leave the country without being noticed. Who better than Blackwell to give me advice on such a delicate question? I called his hotel. A grizzly suffering hibernation interruptus would have passed for an oriental diplomat in comparison with Jimmy Blackwell woken up twice in the same night. As the receiver travelled to his ear he had time to promise me a variety of sexual services I've never experienced before nor ever will.

– You got an illicit haul of sleeping pills you want to sell me or what? he asked once he'd calmed down.

I wasn't in the mood for wisecracks. I got right to the serious stuff.

– I've got to get back to New York pronto, Jimmy, but without going through a French airport, or even a kosher customs check. What's your advice?

– You sure lead an exciting life, he couldn't but remark. Mr Daredevil himself, aren't you. So you've given up the idea of smuggling somebody else through? More fun going solo?

– For now, yes, I said evasively.

But he didn't try to pump me any more. He wouldn't have got much out of me anyway, he saw that right away.

– Listen, the easiest thing is to catch a flight in Brussels. You take an express train, and you cross the frontier, usually without a hitch.

– What do you mean by usually?

– I've done it a hundred times. They hardly look at your passport, especially if you're American. Take a morning train, first class, they're full of businessmen commuting.

– What time are the trains?

– The first's at 7.10, but I don't think I'll have time to

187

deliver your ticket to the hotel, I have to be at Roissy at 8, he said sarcastically. But I can tell you the station: Gare du Nord, the taxis all know it.

– Thanks, Jimmy, I'm in a helluva jam, but I'm really sorry to be such a pain.

– That's okay, that's okay, you can buy me a blow-out dinner in New York, he said, giving me his number in the States. There's a daily flight that leaves Brussels for New York around one in the afternoon. It's a quiet period just now so you shouldn't have any trouble getting a seat. What I can do for you if you like is make you a reservation from Paris, is that okay?

– Sure is, Jimmy, it's really nice of you.

– Okay, TWA Brussels. I'll put you in Ambassador class, like when you came.

– That's great.

I guessed Belmont wouldn't have been in the mood to pop for first class. The operation hadn't actually been an all-out success. I sang Blackwell's praises, wishing him a pleasant trip, first to dreamland, then on his Jumbo. He wished me likewise on my own return home. For the next wake-up call I moved on to Harry, who wasn't asleep. He was breathless even.

– Doing your exercises or what, I said by way of an opener.

– Precisely, old pal. Keeping my pecker in shape.

Harry was very fond of fine wine and subtle humour. He got his breath back.

– What about you, coming or going?

I skipped a tempting wisecrack that occurred, even though it would have gotten a laugh.

– I'm leaving. Finish your vacation without me, in an hour or so I'll be *persona non grata* round here.

– What are you talking about? Been up to more trouble, Sam?

188

– You could call it that. A rat and a whale are both animals. The only difference is their size. But don't ask me to go into details, you've already got something in hand.

But Harry had quit joking.

– Is there anything I can do? he asked anxiously.

– Nothing at all. Give me a call as soon as you get back; I'll be able to fill you in then. I think you might even be interested.

He was still concerned, and kept telling me to take care. I asked him to give my regards to his latest and hung up. There was only Cardier left now on my hit-list. He too was awake.

– So there you are! he exclaimed. I've been leaving messages for you all over the place, so nice of you to call.

– I'm sorry, Pierre, but things have been pretty hectic ever since I got here. I haven't had time to call you back.

– You're not the only one. Have you heard about last night's killings in the suburbs?

– No, I declared.

– A shoot-out between two gangs, Alamo-style. I won't tell you about the damage.

– Please, I cut in. I have to leave Paris in a hurry; have you got time to do me a favour?

This obviously made him suspicious.

– Hey now, you're not in . . . .

– Pierre, can you do me a favour?

He knew me well enough to know he wouldn't get a word out of me.

– Okay, Sam. I've got a lot to catch up on with all this business, and I have to leave for the agency in five minutes. What can I do?

– Pick me up at my hotel at 6.30 and take me to the Gare du Nord, it's high time we saw one another.

He burst out laughing.

– You've got some nerve. And I suppose you'll ask me to buy you a ticket. And where to, if it's not being nosey?

– Brussels.

– Lovely city, I lived there for a few . . . .

– There'll be time for that later, Pierre, can you do it or not?

He thought for a bit, working out how to juggle his office schedule.

– Right, I'll get somebody to fill in for an hour; the traffic's okay then. I'll pick you up at the Warwick, yeah?

– Yes, at 6.30 on the dot, my train's at 7.10.

– Fine, that'll give us some time to talk, eh Sam?

– Sure, Pierre, sure. See you then, and thanks.

Everything seemed to be working out okay, and with a bit of luck I'd be in Brussels by noon, and in New York this evening.

It seemed easy, too easy, so I expected trouble.

It's what's kept me alive since way back when.

I went down to reception to settle my bill and leave my bag. I was relieved of the bulk of my remaining cash – something like five times the rent of my New York office – then I crossed back to the lift. I took it – I had nothing left to pay for it with. I went straight to the sixth floor and had my gun in my hand as I waited for the doors to open. The corridor was quiet and empty. I crept along to de Brown's room and lent an ear. I could still afford that. Light filtered under the door, and I guessed there were two of them talking, plus a musical background. But that doesn't make three. I recognised little Joe's voice. The other wasn't

190

Turner's, and it didn't sound like any of the others I'd met. I gave the door a little kick.

– Who's there? de Brown asked.

– Sam Murchison, open up, Joe. You've nothing to be afraid of.

I heard him rush to the door. I pushed it back a little to see who he'd been talking to and put away my Smith & Wesson when I saw it was the drummer.

– Is it just the two of you here?

– Yes, yes, de Brown answered. Where's Maria-Liza? What's going on?

I closed the door fastening the chain, took him by the shoulder and made him sit down.

– I'm going to tell you. You're a grown-up now.

NINETEEN

For a while I thought he was going to go to pieces when he heard the love of his life had died. He beat his head screaming that it wasn't possible and I was lying. He got violent for a little while and wanted to take it out on me, but I soon dissuaded him, taking care not to hurt him. His buddy collapsed too, though for chemical reasons. Joe took a good half hour to calm down, and he was sinking into a deep depression when I decided to give him a good grilling. It's true that objectively I was the only one to blame for the cataclysm he was going through. But from my point of view a lot of the disasters could have been avoided if he'd told me the whole truth instead of beating about the bush. Maria-Liza had been fatally hooked, and I'd never heard of anyone getting that addicted in just two weeks, which was as long as she'd known de Brown. In the end he admitted she'd had a habit before she met him, though not a serious one.

– It took me a . . . (he could hardly get the words out, he was sobbing so much) it took me a while to realise she had a habit. I . . . to begin with . . . I put it down to instability . . . she was . . . she was very unstable, very . . . disturbed.

Maybe she was disturbed because she was getting high. But people always think the opposite; they prefer to ignore the obvious. I think he'd have given anything to save himself this interrogation, especially since he still had some shocks in store.

I hadn't a minute to lose.

– What's done is done, I announced sagely, but you must realise she didn't die by accident.

– If . . . if you . . . it's because of you that . . . .

– Calm down, it's not that simple. There are people around you who didn't think twice about killing her just to stop me from finding out something. They're the ones to blame. Now tell me how you met, and who introduced you.

I had a feeling what the answer would be.

– It was . . . Turner. He . . . he knew her slightly and knew she was a fan. He brought her along one night when we were playing Miami, That's all there is to it.

– It's Turner who pushes the dope in your outfit, it's Turner who introduced you, it's Turner's pals who bumped off Liza. Don't you think that's a little bit *too much*?

He couldn't handle any more, everything was scrambled in his head and the story had taken on proportions that were quite beyond his grasp. I was expecting the cops to turn up any minute, and I wasn't particularly keen for them to get hold of me.

– Did you see Turner after the concert?

– Yes, of course, we came back to the hotel together, he stayed with me for a while telling me not to worry. He must be in his room. I'll . . . I'll . . . .

– We'll go and say good morning.

– What?

– We'll go and wish him good morning, I repeated. At least *I'll* go and wish him good morning, and you can come with me as far as the door and get him to open it.

I'd broken down enough doors for one night.

– I . . . we'll stop the tour . . . I can't go on . . . I don't know . . . .

I didn't bother to tell him the tour already looked done for if only from the legal point of view.

Turner's room was on the same floor, about ten yards along from de Brown's. I motioned him to make as little noise as possible, and it was only when we got to the door that he made up his mind to knock. Turner wasn't asleep and we immediately heard him approaching to ask who was there.

– It's me, Joe, open the door.

The lock turned and I got rid of de Brown, gently but firmly. Turner couldn't have looked more surprised if he'd found himself face to face with the young Brando. His first move was to try to shut the door again, but a nice 44 was stuck in the gap while a mean 357 that he was all to familiar with was looking him straight in the eyes. He was petrified, his eyes bugging out of his head. I pushed him out of the way and slammed the door behind me. His cases were on the bed packed and ready for departure. His finger was on the way out too.

– Going on vacation?

He started stammering and I slapped him to bolster his self-confidence.

– There are two indestructible species on this earth, I told him: cockroaches and me.

He didn't feel any obligation to smile. I took hold of his shirt so roughly that half his collar came away in my hand. I didn't apologise; I grabbed him by the skin without an intermediary.

194

– It's the moment of truth, Turner. Look, I said, pointing to the window, it's dawn. A hesitant dawn was gradually appearing outside.

– You know, I went on, I'm going to make you talk. Nobody's ever resisted me.

He had no doubts about that but words failed him. At that moment, I could have meted out the worst of punishments, so uncontainable was my hatred. I remembered the story about a big dealer the Puerto Ricans had executed in New York as an example six months before. They'd made him eat his balls, and they'd stuffed his eyes up his ass. I hadn't made up my mind to go that far with Turner; I needed to leave him the use of his mouth at least. I kept on hitting him in the face and ribs until I was satisfied he was really terrified. He wasn't very tough and I could sense he was on the verge of flaking out. I opened the window to give him a bit of fresh air and propped him up next to it, wide open, holding him back by the belt. I pushed him forward and caught him by the feet, to improve his circulation. Once his head was out he noticed the abyss below him and nearly went crazy. Fortunately, we were at a back window and there were no witnesses in sight.

– Who are you working for, Turner? What's all this monkey business with the Belmont kid? Hey, do you hear me?

Strangled gurglings came in spasms from his bloated face. I held him in the same position for a few minutes longer then pulled him up to the window-ledge, choking. He could easily have passed himself off as an Indian but I didn't know any Redskin half as detestable as him. He knew I'd reduce him to pulp if he didn't get down to business.

195

– I'll tell you everything, Murchison, but let me live, I beg you, let me live.

I didn't give a damn about his life, but I knew my planned disappearance could be even more complicated if I left a body in the hotel.

– But I don't want to hurt you, Turner, I only want to hear you talk. Talk.

– Okay, okay. I'm working for a very big US drug smuggler who's trying to get his hands on the whole of the east coast territory.

– His name?

– No, I can't tell . . . .

I took another finger at random, and squeezed it like I was making fruit juice. It made him scream.

– No, please, it's Friedman.

Good old Friedman.

– Go on, Turner, you're on the road to redemption.

– Well, the thing is, one of his direct competitors happens to be Belmont, Maria-Liza's father.

That made me sick to my stomach. I'd honestly never have imagined it. In a flash the whole thing became crystal clear, like a prisoner caught escaping a spotlight beam in the middle of the night in the pen.

– Okay, got it, and once little Liza was in your hands she became your pawn, is that it?

– Yeah, that's right, but even de Brown wasn't aware of it. As for Liza, she only knew her father as a respectable businessman, she didn't know his real business.

It was a smart move. You could have called it kidnapping aggravated with blackmail if the kid hadn't been perfectly willing, at least to begin with. Once she was there, it had been easy for Turner and his team to get her hooked like a slave. And that cretin

196

de Brown hadn't caught on, he was so absorbed in his career and his own habit.

– Turn it on, Turner.

By now he would have recited the Bible for me, if I'd had the notion.

– Belmont was trapped, but he was very fond of his daughter. His only solution was to find somebody who'd come and get her. Nobody on this scene would have taken on a contract like that. Friedman is very much respected, and feared. And that included Belmont, who knew his daughter's death warrant was signed if he didn't give in fast. I think he'd have given up his share in the end.

I'd been well and truly had. To tell the truth, nobody had ever managed to manipulate me that much before. The effect was a bitterness I knew I'd have to live with the rest of my life. There were others, though, who looked like they might not go on living. Turner was spared appearing on my brand new list.

– I'm going to spare your life Turner, and I'll even let you in on a secret. Your chips suddenly lost value during the night. Maria-Liza bought it along with some of your bloodhounds. De Brown will know all about it soon and you're in very deep shit. You'll have a lot of trouble finding yourself life insurance in the next few days, and I can tell you I'm happy about that. You're going to disappear, Turner, without looking back and without the teeniest word to your boss. If I ever happen to find out that you've disobeyed me you'd be risking a punishment I couldn't begin to describe. Wherever you are. Is that clear?

He nodded frantically to signal his agreement.

– You're a living piece of scum, Turner, I continued. But you're very lucky you caught me on a good day.

To persuade him, I helped him up and landed him a

197

heavy punch on the bridge of the nose; it split open. He was squealing like a hog when I knocked him to the ground once again and his skull hit the wall. He'd remember me as the vengeful sandman.

TWENTY

I didn't see de Brown again. I'd had it up to here with the whole band. I got my bag from reception and left the hotel. Rather than wait at the entrance I took up a position on the street corner. It was a one-way street, and Cardier would have to go past me. I lit a fresh cigarette and consulted my watch: 6.20. I was feeling dead beat and would have liked a few hours sleep before leaving. Garbage trucks lumbered up the Champs-Elysées by grinding fits and starts. It had stopped raining but it looked like being a cool day, weatherwise anyways. In the distance I heard two sirens getting closer and I made myself scarce, hugging the window of the store selling classy clothes for kiddiwinks. I saw two police cars bombing towards me from further down the avenue. They turned just in front of me and screeched to a stop outside the Warwick. Seven plain clothes piled out and disappeared into the lobby. It was nowhere near de Brown's bedtime, but Turner was due to get woken up. I breathed a sigh of relief that let out a cloud of smoke, and got back to watching out for Cardier. I didn't have long to wait. Five minutes later I spotted him inside an old French jalopy and signalled him not to take the corner.

He claimed I hadn't really changed in all this time and I returned the compliment. He'd put on a bit of weight and lost his hair, but I found his good-humoured nature unchanged.

– Looks like these aren't the ideal circumstances for a reunion, he said.

I acquiesced, with a plea to step on the gas pronto. I had a train to catch, he knew already. After we'd done some reminiscing I could feel him burning with impatience to get to the bottom of why I was in France. He'd honed the suspicions I'd provoked on the phone. And what's more he could update me on the showdown in the suburbs.

– A real slaughter, Sam. Eleven dead. A bunch of bikers against a gang of crooks, most of them vamooshed. Then, into the bargain, some of the crew from a band on tour that's playing in Paris right now. A real shambles.

He finished with a question mark. I couldn't give him any answers. Instead I got him going again, to see who the cops were looking for and where.

– There's talk of an American mixed up with the killings. But either they don't know who he is, or they want to keep it quiet. I can't tell you any more that that, Sam. You wouldn't happen to have any ideas? he probed.

– Listen, Pierre, let's put our cards on the table. I could tell you a story that would put you in line for the Pulitzer Prize, but for the moment I can't say anything. I give you my solemn word I'll call you in two or three days and let you have every last detail. Is that a deal? Of course you'll make sure you keep your source quiet.

– Okay, Sam, it's a deal.

Pierre was a good, fast driver and each street on our

route took us clearer of traffic. He stopped outside the station at 6.50. He did me one last favour by going to the international window to buy my ticket, and reserving me a seat in first class. He came back and gave me the stuff like it was do-or-die.

– You're in luck, he said, it's a TGV, it takes less than two and a half hours to reach Brussels, non-stop. It leaves from platform J, you'd better get a move on.

I piled on the thanks, repeating my promise to call him as soon as I could. I appreciated what he'd done for me. I ran to the train, found my coach and took my place in my compartment among four guys straight from first class, even if it was a class I'd never get into. They all reeked of managing director or sales chief. I put my bag up, having extracted the *New York Times*, which I hadn't had time to open. But it wasn't that old. The *Times* made a good impression on them, as if this meaningless sign showed them we spoke the same language. I greeted the assembled company with a smile that would have got me a top job in PR with the Moonies. Before I sat down I dropped into the toilet and hid my 357 there using all my practised skill for camouflage. It seemed wise. I went back and settled down among my travelling companions, who all had long faces – a mixture of sleepiness, cuckoldry, persistent haemorrhoids and liver trouble. I checked the soles of my shoes, but I hadn't stepped in anything. I took out my pack of Winstons and offered them to these bozos, though it went against the grain. You have to know how to behave in company now and then. There was only one that accepted; he gave me a strained smile and introduced himself after I lit his cigarette. He was the boss of a Franco-Belgian plumbing company, specialising in washing machine outflow pipes. The guy led an exciting life, non-stop

201

between Paris and Brussels, probably looking for new outlets for his unique shit pipes. He told me about market trends broken down from the latest figures, problems with the workforce in France and Belgium (I could have given him a working over myself) and other facts that would have even the most determined crossword enthusiast dying of boredom. He had a notion he'd move into the US market some day, but I told him it was pretty crowded. I myself was on a trip to Europe to find a new strain of galley slave – the only way of loosening the Japanese grip on the industry; there you are, things were a lot more complicated than they used to be. We harked back to the golden age of post-war industry, the era of reconstruction, and he said he'd be willing to relive those years, even if it meant enormous sacrifice. I kept myself going like this for a good hour and a half, welcoming our neighbours with open arms when they'd warmed up enough to join the conversation. This way, when customs opened the door of our compartment, they found a lovely bunch of gentlemen forging the future together. They were the Air and Frontier Police, French, and they scarcely glanced at our documents. My pipe buddy told me the customs service initials: P.A.F. In French this spelled out a word he translated for me as NUTS. This sent him into fits of laughter. The Belgian customs had the pleasure of meeting the wild and woolly businessmen's club too, and their reaction was bewilderment. Their amazement re-ignited our hilarity afresh, and after they left he told me the Belgians were jerks. I pointed out that everybody's somebody's jerk, and he took it very well. I'd managed to cross the frontier and I silently congratulated Blackwell on his idea.

There was a little less than an hour of the journey to

go and hunger was gnawing at my insides. I asked the other guys whether there was a restaurant car. They said I'd find a buffet car a few cars down. I took off before it occurred to them to go with me, and wolfed some hardboiled eggs and black coffee for want of anything more appealing. I stayed there for a while, smoking as I watched the scenery and the cows watching the train go by. This gave me a terrific idea.

I wasn't at all happy with how things had gone and I was thinking of a smart way of winding them up neatly. I glimpsed the shape of a city on the horizon. I looked at my watch. It had to be Brussels. I stopped in at the toilet to reclaim my weapon , and returned to my seat. My absence had sobered things up. I took care not to get them going again.

It was just after 9.30 when the train pulled into the central station. I was doing good, and I knew it. I left my companions with no regrets and legged it down the platform. Usually, you get on a train at a point that leaves you with miles to walk when you arrive. That's the way it was again this time. When I left the station I hailed a taxi and told him to take me to the airport. I opened my window wide to wake me up a bit and what came back at me was an overwhelming smell of chocolate. There must have been a factory round there. Funnily enough, it perked me up. I had forty minutes in that car, listening to the driver's shrieks, since every car that passed called for one of his freaky *'potferdoum'* or *'potferdek'*'s, words whose translation I happily did without.

Even a Mongolian would have had trouble missing the airport – *zaventem* in the local lingo. The symbol of a huge plane left little doubt. I changed back what I had in French francs for good old Yankee dollars, then went to expedite my ticket. Blackwell had kept his promise. There was a seat waiting for me, and I charged it against my original ticket and even got some change. I had two hours to kill clear, and I took myself off to the bar. I gave Belinda a call to bring her up to date and tell her about my imminent return. I made a point of asking her to reach Belmont, and tell him to head for New York as soon as possible to collect his daughter.

– Collect his daughter, Sam?

– Yes, along with a gift, a souvenir of Paris.

She didn't press me any further. While I had her on the line I told her to contact Joe so he would keep his evening free. I had my heart set on celebrating my return to New York. I bought a few papers, including *La Libre Belgique*, not for the words but for the pictures. It was a good idea, for inside on page 3 I found a terrific shot of the Rattlesnakes' pit, next to several graphic pics of the stiffs. No captions, just faces. I skimmed the paper looking for familiar names, mine for a start, but didn't find any.

I ordered myself a slap-up breakfast. Coffee again, ham, eggs and fruit. I counted the minutes until boarding and around the eighty-sixth I had the pleasure of hearing the announcement. I went through passport control without a hitch and was shortly planted in a comfortable seat right by a window. When we took off I gave a little wave to the Old World, downed a double whisky and, after one last cigarette, covered my eyes with a sleep mask. I don't think anyone ever fell asleep so fast. Except to sleep the sleep of death.

TWENTY-ONE

Belinda wouldn't have welcomed me any differently if I'd been away partying for two years in one of the world's hotspots. She wouldn't have welcomed me any differently if we'd been engaged, and I had to start by calming her down and putting her, gently, back in her place. Sometimes this girl goes completely mental when she sees me, which isn't at all unusual, but it gets on my nerves in the end. And though the sleep I'd got on the plane relaxed me, it had left me on edge.

I waited outside the airport while she got her car out of the lot: an old Mercury 77 that was beginning to feel its age but at least when you were in it you could stretch your legs without having them go through the floor. Naturally, Belinda inundated me with questions. I told her no more than when I'd left. I'd let her have the details once everything was sorted out. She asked me about Paris as if she was planning to write a travel guide, and I cut short the inevitable 'city of contrasts' to ask her if she'd managed to speak to Belmont.

– Sure, Sam. He's very pleased, and he'll be in New York tomorrow morning. I've made him an appointment at the office.

This was fine by me. She assured me she'd followed my instructions and hadn't set foot there. But she'd picked up the messages on the answering machine. I'd been offered two cases, one of them connected with the Triads. It looked interesting.

– No news of our visitors, I asked.

– No, nothing since you left. So you really were right by the Champs-Elysées? Tell me about it, Sam.

– Later, sweetie, I'm a bit tired, I lied.

I was glad to be back home. There's no denying that when you leave the States even for a few days it's good to get back on the highway into Manhattan. It makes Shea Stadium look almost pretty. Well, for that you have to be abroad for at least a week. To celebrate I turned on the radio and lit a cigarette. It was mush, as usual, but I was surprised to find, strangely, that I didn't mind it. With the time difference it was only early afternoon and the sun was shining. For a few moments it felt as if I'd dreamt everything that had happened, or that it had happened far, far away, on another planet.

The traffic on the highway was light, and we took less than half an hour to get to the mid-town tunnel. I directed Belinda to my apartment, but to her great disappointment I didn't invite her up. I didn't want to kindle the slightest spark of hope in her hungry heart. Nobody had been there since my night with Hammer, but I wasn't complaining about the mess. I felt as glad as a wild beast making it back to his lair after the hunt. I knew though that I still had some big game to bag. This image made me hungry and I went down to the local deli to get myself a turkey sandwich, some broccoli salad, a few ice cold Budweisers and the *Post*. I guzzled the whole lot, except for the newspaper, half watching the twelve thousandth showing of *MASH*, waiting in vain for Hot Lips to appear. I ran myself a deep bath. Sometimes you have to know how to take your time. After a nice close shave I gave Joe a call at his office. Belinda had let him know I'd be back in town all right. He'd made sure he was free that evening – not that night, he emphasised – and he would drop by my apartment to pick me up at 7 sharp. He was one of the few people who knows the telephone wasn't invented for spouting your life story, and I loved him for it. I heated up some coffee and lay down on my bed, which still had Hammer's sweetish odour on it. I thought about her briefly, promising myself to track her down soon for another session, then buried myself in the newspaper, starting with the sports page. The TV was pumping out its usual mindless crud. Game shows followed soaps which followed game shows. It would take a nuclear war to make them change their schedules, but it was all the same to me. I idled the hours away like this, having a few beers, until 6.30, then I thought I'd drop in at the Tonkin'. I parcelled up my dirty laundry and threw on an old pair of jeans and a T-shirt. They all said I should have let them know when I was coming back. It would have given them the time to get a little party together. I promised to do better next time and collected two suits and three ultrawhite shirts.

Back in the apartment, I put on my favourite suit, the plain black alpaca, and set it off with a white shirt and a black tie with a thin red stripe. Looking like that I felt at home again, and I was just hesitating between two different hats when the ground floor entryphone rang. I recognised Joe's unmistakable voice and told him to come up. He hugged me furiously, as if I'd come back from beyond the grave. It made him delirious to see me back in one piece.

– You know I get bored when you're not around, he told me affectionately.

– We'll drink to that, Joe, I've got a bit of cash and we'll spend the evening getting rid of it.

I'd given some thought to the details, and I put them to him.

– We'll start off at Peter Lueger's, then the Old Town Bar and we'll take in a club. What do you think?

I saw his eyes sparkle.

– That sounds great, Sam, I couldn't have planned it better myself, I sure couldn't.

If there was anybody I could spill the beans to, it was Joe. We were sitting in Lueger's, on the other side of Brooklyn Bridge, in front of two huge T-bones, with potato salad and beer. It's one of my favourite eateries in the whole world; they've got the very best meat and they cook it the way you want. Of course, they don't give it away, but it's a cruel world. Joe didn't look very surprised by what I told him. He said the drug scene was really something else, he'd heard some pretty juicy stories before.

– By the way, I've been offered a case, it's the Chinese this time.

– The Tongs! he exclaimed. Forget it. I'm telling you as a friend. Those guys are wackoes. At the moment they're busy playing with their M16s: Chinese, Vietnamese, Koreans all knocking one another off, and recently, it seems, the Japanese too. They make the Columbians and Puerto Ricans look like babysitters.

I found all this appealing, but I'd think it over later. Joe filled me roughly in on how the coke market worked. Basically it had assumed the proportions of a massive industry.

– You've still got to be careful, Sam, you don't know who you're dealing with, and you can't even know whether the case is finished with.

That didn't really bother me. I just wanted to settle some personal scores, not become the lone avenger of the naked city. Each to his own. We got to more private matters, like delightful Ruth's state of health.

– She's all the better for my convincing her you were away for a while, he said. If you keep a low profile life will be plain sailing.

It was hard to think of myself as a hydro-electric dam.

– Watch out for the currents, Joe, I cautioned him.

As usual, soon we got restless and needed some fresh air. As planned, I took Joe along to the Old Town Bar, on 18th Street, between Park and Broadway. It really was the oldest New York bar, and it would have been a perfect tourist trap if the owner had had the slightest notion of attracting new customers. I was crazy about this place – I'd spent more evenings there than there are lawyers in the Yellow Pages. It was practically empty, as it nearly always is, and it still made you feel as if life had stood still at the turn of the century. We put away nine or ten Wild Turkeys and went on jawing about nothing much, wisecracking with Buck, the barman, who joined us occasionally in our descent of the rapids. Ruth was now bound to suspect her husband of drinking alone, the worst thing of all!

I thought some more fresh air would do us good, and I took Joe a few blocks down to a club where I used to be a regular a few years back. I figured we were ready to listen to some music, and *good* music, by Christ. We were in luck, for tonight it was Buster Pointdexter, a terrific cabaret singer who belts out blues, ballads and standards all evening as if he was alone in the Grand Canyon. A few beers more got the better of Joe, and after joining in a rousing chorus of 'New York Is My Town' ("cos when you leave New York/you ain't going nowhere') which I found particularly apt, I put him in a taxi and paid the fare up front to ensure he'd get home quietly. I straightened the angle of my hat and set off home whistling.

TWENTY-TWO

I woke up with no jet lag at 9.30 and called Belinda right away to ask her to get Belmont's bill ready, and to put it with the messages I'd had while I was away.

– Put it all in the letterbox at the office then go back home. I just want you to drop in this afternoon to tidy up a bit.

She couldn't understand why I was keeping her away from my meeting with Belmont, but I didn't feel there was any need to tell her. I spent a while dismantling and cleaning my Smith & Wesson, and reloaded it with ordinary ammo as I drank truckloads of steaming hot coffee. I opened the blind. A spring sun flooded the street with white light, and it looked like the start of a perfect day. It was my turn for a thorough clean-up, undismantled, then I trotted down to the corner coffee shop for some eggs. I loafed around reading the gossip in the *Post* and smoking a few cigarettes without watching the time. Life in New York was as harrowing as ever, going by what I had in front of me. A gang of women had just kidnapped, raped, tortured and finally killed an Italian stock-broker of sixty-two. The gang was run by a female monster weighing something like three hundred

211

pounds. Elsewhere there was a reward of 10,000 dollars offered to anybody whose help would lead to the arrest of a cop killer. Nothing out of the ordinary.

At 11.15 sharp I left Joe's Junior. I thought I'd walk to my office. I got there at 11.40 and picked up Belinda's envelope. It felt like I hadn't been there for centuries and I needed a few minutes to get used to being there and the sight of everything. I'd bought a bottle of Jack Daniels on the way and I wiped two glasses clean as I waited for Belmont. I couldn't hear any hammering from the building next door; they must have been taking a break. I was lost in contemplation of the traffic when there was a knock at the door.

– Come in, I answered, with a great sense of timing.

There was Belmont, wiping his brow. His face was flushed.

– Your elevator's stuck, he said, out of breath, you should call the maintenance people.

I could have fixed it myself faster, because I was the one who'd jammed it at the top floor.

– How are you, Mr Belmont? Take a seat, I said, first holding out my hand politely, then an armchair. I sat on the corner of my desk.

– Where's Maria-Liza, Mr Murchison?

– My secretary's looking after her. She took her to spend the night at her place, and I'm expecting them any minute. Will you have a drink? I've only got whisky.

– That's fine, but just a drop, it's still a bit early.

It's a lot later than you think, I said to myself as I poured our drinks.

– So, he continued, everything turned out okay?

– For the best, Mr Belmont, for the best. Here, I've had your bill made up. Six days on the job at $125, that comes to $750, plus $62 in taxes, which makes a total of $812. The cash for the Paris expenses just covered everything. Your daughter's very extravagant, as you probably know. But I've plenty of receipts.

– Oh yes, he agreed, writing out a cheque in my name. Don't I know it.

– Tut tut, you're certainly partly to blame, Mr Belmont.

– You don't raise an eagle in a rabbithole. Do you know what I mean?

I wasn't sure I'd fully grasped this dazzling analogy. I brought him back down to earth.

– Tell me, Mr Belmont, do you know your daughter takes drugs?

His face assumed a dismissive expression. An indulgent daddy kind of look.

– Oh yes, I had an idea, she smokes, doesn't she?

This guy obviously thought I was a retard.

– Worse than that, Mr Belmont.

This time he feigned astonishment.

– What do you mean by that?

– Harder drugs than grass. You know, the American scourge, as they say in the papers. What's it called now? Cocaine?

– No, you're joking?

It's true I was probably giving him a little teasing smile.

– Not at all, I'm dead serious. To be honest, you should keep an eye on her. She's endangering her health you know? Anyway, I can guarantee she won't get any worse.

He shot me a scared, suspicious look. This time he raised his voice.

– What are you talking about? Where's my daughter? I want to see my daughter immediately.

213

I swallowed half the contents of my glass and calmly lit a cigarette.

– She's on her way, relax. Listen, while you're here I mustn't forget to pass on Benett Friedman's regards.

This took all the colour out of his cheeks; he turned as white as my molars.

– I . . . I . . . know nobody of that name, he spluttered.

– Give me a break, Belmont.

I was still smiling at him when in one marvellously adroit move, I pulled my 357 from behind my back and struck it up his schnozz. I could feel myself losing my cool.

– What's going on? What are you playing at? Are you crazy, Murchison?

I gave him a couple of slaps to shut him up for the moment.

– You're the one who's crazy, Belmont. You don't know what it means to try and make of fool of Sam Murchison. I don't know a single guy alive who can say he's done it. And rest assured I know all about your little trafficking business, so you can spare me any crap.

He stared at me wide-eyed, stammering. Then he started vibrating like crazy.

– Where, where . . . is my daughter?

– In the morgue, in Paris. I didn't have a coffin handy to bring her back.

He collapsed, his eyes filled with tears. I pulled him back up without ceremony.

– Don't worry, you'll be with her soon, I said soothingly.

I released the trigger of the Magnum and brought it level with his mouth. He was on the verge of apoplexy

214

– he knew his time was up. He played his last card, hoping to soften me.

– How much, Mu . . . Mu . . . Murchison? How much? A hundred thousand dollars. Two . . . two hundred

I pretended not to have heard.

– If you want to soften me up, Belmont, I'm like raw meat, you need to hit me with something big.

– Three . . . three hundred . . . .

I pushed my gun in his mouth and pulverised his front teeth, which were false anyway. It made an unpleasant noise and extra difficult for him to get the words out. He was crazy with fear, and it didn't surprise me when he began choking and clutching at his chest, then fell backwards with a grimace of pure horror. Sweat was pouring out of him and he was turning a yellowish colour as he gasped for breath, gulping at the air he so badly needed.

I watched him writhing on the floor for at least a minute, knocking into everything around him. His face was paralysed with pain and he let out a harsh rattling noise. I wished him a speedy recovery as I finished off my glass, and my wish was granted. After one last jerk, he arched his back and fell in a lifeless heap. That made one reptile less on earth.

I put my gun away and went and sat down at Belinda's desk. I scribbled a note telling her to stay on vacation until the following week, and to call me at my apartment if she needed any cash. I decided to leave her my home number, knowing that this small gesture would brighten up her life for a month. It wouldn't be too difficult to have my number changed if she became too intrusive. I rang the local precinct to send an ambulance, and told them about the cardiac case dead beside me. Then I took another sheet of paper and wrote a note for Harry's attention, pinning it on Belmont's jacket.

Harry,
This is the body of Glenn Belmont, managing director of Belmont Inc., also one of the biggest coke importers in the US. He died in my office, as you'll see in your report, and as you'll see from the autopsy, I didn't lay a hand on him. (Harry would forgive me this venial sin.) *You'll get some very interesting information from a certain Jack Turner, who I suppose is somewhere in Europe on the lam, if he's still alive, or else from Benett Friedman, World Talent Agency, New York, another big fish in the same game as Belmont, if he's STILL alive. Everything depends on exactly how long your vacation lasted. Did it end well? I'm dying to hear all about it!*

All the best

Sam Murchison.

I left my office door open with the cops in mind, and liberated the elevator. I'd be back to lock up later on. But for the moment there was only one thing I wanted to do: take a stroll through the streets of Manhattan.
Round Chinatown way, maybe.